Island Wildlife:
Exiles, Expats and Exotic Others

Robert Friedman

Aignos Publishing
an imprint of Savant Books and Publications
Honolulu, HI, USA
2018

Published in the USA by Aignos Publishing LLC
an imprint of Savant Books and Publications LLC
2630 Kapiolani Blvd #1601
Honolulu, HI 96826
http://www.aignospublishing.com

Printed in the USA

Edited by Eleonor Gardner
Cover by Eleonor Gardner

13-digit ISBN: 9780997002072

First Edition: February 2018
Library of Congress Control Number: 2018931279

May 29, 2018

To Eduardo,

¡Viva Puerto Rico!

Dedication

To Donna, Maddy and Lizzy

Bob Friedman

Chapter 1

Bernardo, relieving himself in the middle of the night, caught the scene from the second-floor bathroom window. A full moon shed pale light on the patio.

With a towel around his head and a sheet around his body, the guy looked like a Thuggee out of *Gunga Din.* He climbed the crossbars supporting the ten-foot link-fence, unfurled the towel and bunched it on the metal spikes. Hoisting himself over, he scrambled down the chain links and whisked bare-footed across the patio.

Here we go again!

Bernardo rushed to the top of the staircase, then crept down. He heard the intruder working the patio door leading into the lobby. Why the hell hadn't he installed the drop bolt for the door as he had meant to do for weeks, after the last attempted break-in?

The guy pushed hard and the door, only locked from the other side with a flimsy hook-and-eye, flew open, the loose metal hook popping out of the wood onto the ground. The intruder entered the lobby. Bernardo went back up to the top steps; he didn't know if the guy was armed. The guy tried the door to the room across from the front desk. The room was unoccupied. There was only a bed, a dresser, chair and empty desk in there.

The intruder tried the doors of the other room down the hallway of the guesthouse and found them locked. Bernardo again started down the steps to get to his office. The guy turned toward the front desk and Bernardo backed up again to the top of the staircase.

He hadn't locked the door to the office behind the front desk. *Damn!*

He crouched down on the top step; he could see the front desk, see the guy go into the office, hear drawers opening and closing.

He had to get down there, into the safe*!*

Heart whacking away once again. Nerves twitching along his arms. The kids. Damn! Get those locks! Put barbed wire on top of the goddamn gates!

After some minutes, the guy came out, bare-chested, wearing only jockey shorts. The booty, which Bernardo was sure included his new IBM computer, was wrapped and tied up in the sheet and cradled in the thief's skinny arms as he stumbled out of the office. Bernardo crept down the stairs one more time. He saw the thief heading for the front door. He heard the lock there being unbolted—and in his mind's eye, saw the sonovabitch facing the wrought-iron gate bought after the last break-in.

The Gate jiggled, got smacked in frustration and then the thief turned back and stumbled out the door leading to the patio.

Bernardo shot down the rest of the steps and into the office, spun the numbers on his safe, retrieved the .45 and rushed into the patio. The guy was at the foot of the fence, gazing up open-mouthed, wondering how he was going to get over with the stuff wrapped in the sheet.

He finally decided to untie the sheet, took from it Bernardo's old Bulova watch from Cuba that had been left on the office desk, and the autographed baseball cards of Roberto Clemente and Luis Tiant that Bernardo had bought at an auction to give to Pablito for his birthday next week.

The would-be thief looked down sadly at the computer, which he couldn't get over the fence. Slipping the watch and the cards inside his jockey shorts, he began to climb back up the crossbars. He hoisted one foot over the towel-covered spikes, started down the fence, found himself staring through the links into the muzzle of a gun.

Bernardo noted the track marks on the guy's arms. Poor jerk. Still...

He pointed the pistol between the junkie's eyes.

"Give me that watch and those baseball cards, *cabrón,* or you die."

The junkie inhaled quickly. His eyes shot open; his nostrils trembled, as though a sneezing fit was coming on; his lips puckered. He dug into his shorts, tossed the watch, then both cards, over the fence. He tumbled back onto the sand, lurched across the beach, fell, picked himself up and stumbled toward the ocean's breaking waves.

The next morning, Bernardo Alvarez collected the newspapers outside the front door, and placed a copy of *The New York Times* in front of the door to Fred Anderson's room. He went out to the patio with the other *Times,* the *San Juan Star* and *El Nuevo Día* and sat at one of the round wrought-iron mesh tables. All six of the tables and the chairs, he saw, could use another whitewash. The table umbrellas, piled in a corner with the folded up beach chairs under a tall, mango tree, were all in good shape, ready to block out the sun for the tourists, whenever the hell they started coming down. He glanced at the well-stacked, five-stooled bar by the gate to the beach. Perry did a great job taking care of it and the little kitchen in the back, where soups and sandwiches and coffee, etc. was served. Maybe a raise for Perry, once the season began.

Carmencita, who was cleaning up the kitchen, brought

Bernardo his early morning demitasse of *café Cubano* from the expresso machine, along with toasted-and-buttered *pan de agua.*

His kids came through the broken door to the patio.

"Bye, *Papi.*"

"Bye, *Papi.*"

"Did you both have your cereal?"

"*Sí.*"

"*Sí.*"

"Pablito, I want you home right after school, we have to go to the dentist, to get your braces fixed."

"*Sí, Papi.*"

"After classes, I'm going with Patricia to Plaza Las Americas," said Anita, walking out to where he sat. "Is that all right? Could you pick us up at the mall later?"

Anita cradled her books. She wore a crisp white blouse beneath her blue plaid school jumper. Her long black hair fanned out over her shoulders. Bernardo noticed she had lost most of the chubbiness in her face. Her high cheekbones began to give form to her face. She had brought out the beautiful blue-green of her eyes with green eye shadow. His little girl in the school uniform was nearing womanhood, turning into a real beauty—in the image of Pilar. His heart tightened.

"All right, *mi amor,*" Bernardo said. "I'll get you on our

way home from the dentist. Be in front of Penney's at five."

Anita kissed her father on his forehead. She and her brother left to walk the few blocks to school.

He didn't say anything to anyone about last night. As soon as he finished his coffee and read the papers, he would buy an extra strong lock for the side door and barbed wire to put on the top of the fence. The crime was getting ridiculous.

He heard the phone on the front desk ring and went back inside. A call from the states. It was a cancellation of a two-week reservation. Bad news in the off-season. The rental would have allowed him to pay several outstanding bills. Bernardo took a deep breath again, exhaled slowly. He returned to the patio and had another strong Cuban coffee.

That afternoon, Bernardo bought and installed the new lock, then took his son to the orthodontist. Before they left the office, while he was making a future appointment, the secretary said: "Should I mail out again your bill from last month or would you prefer to pay it now?"

"Didn't I…?" Knowing damn well he hadn't. He wrote out a check, not sure he had enough in the bank to cover it.

He dropped Pablito at a friend's house, then picked up his daughter and her friend at Plaza Las Americas, the huge indoor mall packed, as always, with shoppers, strollers, idlers and others. Bernardo remembered his days in Havana when the outdoor squares around town were the places to meet and greet and sit and stare. Not everyone was out buying, buying, buying.

As much as Anita was a budding beauty, Patricia was an awkward, unformed teenager. Tall, skinny, cheeks pimpled, she spoke to Bernardo in a whispery voice as though to call as little attention to herself as possible, putting herself on hold until her body matured and her face cleared. Before they left, Anita convinced her father to go with them to a costume jewelry kiosk and buy her a peace-sign necklace. Bernardo coaxed Patricia to choose a necklace, also. She too chose a peace sign and thanked Bernardo shyly. He started to put it around her neck and she turned beet-red and began trembling.

"Don't, Dad!" Anita said.

"What?"

Anita took the necklace from her father and handed it to Patricia, who put it in her book bag, then began crying.

"Patricia doesn't like to be touched."

For Christsake!

They took the sobbing Patricia home. Anita walked her to the front door, then got back in the car with tears in her eyes. Now what? "What's the matter, *mi amor?'*

"Papi, why is it people don't see things as they really are?"

"Like what?"

"Well, like the boys at my school. They're always talking

7

to me, but they never talk to Patricia. They ignore her because she's not pretty. She's got this complex. I'm sorry about what happened at the mall. I should have said something. She's so nice, and when she's with me, she's really smart and funny, you know? Why don't other people see what's inside her? She suffers a lot."

"She's just going through a difficult stage. She'll be okay, you'll see."

It may only scar her for life, Bernardo didn't add.

When Bernardo and Anita arrived at the guesthouse, they went up to their apartment where Bernardo napped for an hour, then picked up Pablito from his friend's house. While Anita and Pablito did their homework, he prepared a dinner of pan-fried minute steaks, rice and black beans, and salad.

Bernardo and his children lived in three adjoining rooms on the second floor of the guesthouse. When he had taken over the place, he moved walls and converted the rooms into an apartment and installed a kitchen. You walked into a living room with an alcove kitchen and a dining area. Pablito slept on a convertible sofa in the living room. Past the kitchen to the right was the bathroom, to the left was Anita's bedroom. Bernardo 's room was at the rear. From the bathroom window was a wide, gleaming view of the ocean.

Besides the apartment, there were fifteen rooms in the

Solimar Guesthouse. Four were rented on a monthly basis by boarders: Fred Anderson, Burt Cherry, Don Cisco and Miss Silva. Three other rooms were now being occupied by tourists. The rest of the rooms were empty, and there were few advanced bookings through the summer.

After the kids got to bed, Bernardo went downstairs and made sure the patio gate leading to the beach was locked. The only customer at the bar was Paco, who spent his nights moving from bar to bar along the beach, haranguing tourists in a sarcastically friendly way, then letting them buy him drinks. The bars were now bereft of tourists, which gave Paco little recourse but to nurse his beers at one place each night. Paco was a barfly; he needed to drink, but he needed more to talk. Right now, he was relating to Perry, the bartender, how his Army MOS in Vietnam had been "infantryman/throat slasher." He had developed a skill and passion for ripping open throats of gooks, he told Perry, detailing his craft.

"So this slant is gurgling and the blood is spurting out like he's getting off through his throat with red come and it splashes onto my face and it tastes sweet and sticky, which really pissed me off, so first I hacked off an ear, then..."

Bernardo went behind the bar and poured himself a cognac and sat at one of the tables. At least five more months until the tourist season began and business would pick up again. It would be touch-and-go until then. Tomorrow, he would sit down and go through the bills and pay what he could; though after writing out that check to the orthodontist, he doubted if he could pay many more. Still, he would put the bills in order when he had to pay them. He'd do it first thing in the morning.

Paco continued his war stories, getting louder. "The most fun was to come on them sleeping in their hooches, you know? You slit 'em from ear to ear and their eyes open and the look they give ya, it's so fuckin' funny, you piss your pants..."

At eleven that night, Bernardo told Perry to close the bar. Paco swung out of his seat. He walked over to Bernardo. "What's the matter? Why are you closing up early? You got something against the local clientele?"

Bernardo looked up into Paco's beefy, sweating face. He was smiling and his small, slanted eyes were gleaming like he was his usual kidding self, but Bernardo recognized the essential meanness of the man.

"You got something against guys who fought in Nam? Hey, I know you're from Cuba. What are you, a commie or a *gusano?"*

"Leave," Bernardo said in a low voice, but with hardness in his eyes.

"Yeah? You want to make me leave?" Paco was weaving back and forth.

Bernardo pushed his chair back and got to his feet. He was half a foot taller than Paco, whose massive stomach stretched beneath a tight black polo shirt. "Leave. Get out. I don't want you in here anymore. I'm tired of your nonsense."

Paco looked up at Bernardo. "You don't want to hear the truth. That's tough! Nobody kicks me out of nowhere. Least of all, you, you commie sonovabitch!" Paco pulled his beefy arm back. Perry slammed through the swinging door at the end of the bar and grabbed Paco's fist and twisted his arm behind his back, forcing him across the patio.

"Fuckin' *gusano!*" Paco screamed as he was pushed through the lobby and out the front door.

"Sorry, boss," Perry said to Bernardo as he returned to cleaning up glasses behind the bar. "The war messed up his head. He's been eighty-sixed from most of the bars in the Condado and Isla Verde. I'll make sure he stays away from here, too."

Bernardo shrugged, then nodded.

Perry finished cleaning up and left. Bernardo brought the bottle of cognac to his table. He poured a generous amount, sniffed it and drank.

He thought of how Pilar's full-bodied beauty had sweetened his life. How that image remained even after she had been eaten away. How each day the shock was renewed when he saw her disappearing; how great weights lodged in his body and how his mind could not accept that the afterimage was no longer the reality. But now, this afterimage *was* the reality.

Pilar was gone. Now, all he wanted was the sea, the sun, his kids, nothing else. Well, other things of course. He had to live and make a living—for Anita and Pablito. He had to manage the guesthouse—life.

He stood and shook himself, like a dog trying to recover from a sudden drenching.

He put the cognac bottle back behind the bar and returned to his room.

As he lay in bed, he saw her again, voluptuous, as bright and as intense as the New York skyline across from the Promenade in Brooklyn Heights where she had lived. She had been born and raised in that city and could be as tough and to the point as it was, but she was also nurturing and resourceful, shrewd and humane—a Latin woman.

New York, August, 1971. Hotter than any day in Havana. A tall and shiny city, but filthy. Yet more than anything, exciting. Driving a cab, getting to know Red Hook from Greenpoint, Hempstead from Highbridge, the Bronx from Bensonhurst. Seeing and hearing, live, in the Village the jazz stars he had gotten to love by recordings, Miles Davis, Bill Evans, the MJQ. Movies at the Thalia, the classics, from "Children of Paradise" to "Gunga Din." Plays off off-

Broadway. And meeting Pilar at the dance at the Roosevelt Hotel. That beautiful satiny red dress. What a knockout! Walks along the Promenade. Pilar says she never gets over the view nor does Havana-raised he. Those emerald eyes opening wide in wonder and creasing in skepticism almost at the same time. That smile reflecting the warmth of her soul. A hot temper, flying off at a perceived injustice, without all the facts. So what? A warm soul, a generous heart, a luscious body—all the clichés to truly describe the woman he had lost way too soon.

Honeymoon in Puerto Rico, where Pilar's mother was born. The family all over them. The beaches, the salt smell in the air, the adobo, sazón, achobe *in the food, the Spanish fortresses on the bay and the old parts of the city, a lot like Havana. The move when Anita was four months old.*

Living in the Old City. Working for a tourism company driving passengers from the ship piers to the rain forest and the island beaches and the luxury hotels. Swearing his allegiance to the United States in the federal courthouse in the Old City; walking outside the building and seeing other recent escapees—parakeets warbling in the trees in the little plaza there. Passing the exam at the Architects, Engineers and Surveyors Association, allowed to practice engineering again.

Her coal-black hair falls over her eyes and then she

throws her head back as he kisses her ivory neck and her mouth opens to reveal slightly spaced front teeth—a perfect imperfection. Tears form and he kisses her and tastes the tastes in her mouth and enters her and digs deeper into her, deeper in passion, deeper in anger and frustration, deeper in love, and she put her arms around his neck and pulls him to her and he can feel her breath on his ear as she convulses beneath him and her moaning turns into the moans coming from him and his body tingles down his legs to his toes.

He wiped himself with a towel. He had relieved his body, but not a great part of his soul.

The next morning, Bernardo stood at the espresso machine downing the syrupy liquid, thinking of it as a life-sustaining transfusion. Then, he returned to his office and went through the stack of bills, writing out checks for those that could be covered by his dwindling bank account. About noon, the hardware store truck arrived. Two men installed the barbed wire, intertwining the spikes in the wire. After the installation was complete, Bernardo drove his 10-year-old Plymouth to the supermarket and did a week's worth of shopping. He spent the rest of the day on repairs—attaching a missing showerhead, replacing torn window screens, plastering and repainting two rooms on the first floor. He picked up his kids from the homes of friends. At dusk, he put on a dark long-sleeved shirt and gardening gloves and went after the mud-built wasp nest he had spied on a bush right under the window of one of the rooms he had been painting. He put a large, dark green plastic trash bag over the nest and quickly tied off the top. Then he put the bag in a pail of water and dropped a large rock on the bag. He'd deposit the bag into the garbage bin in the morning.

After making a dinner of pork chops, white rice, black beans and a salad for himself and the kids, Bernardo took an evening walk down to the beach, accompanied by Billie Holiday singing on his new Walkman. The moon laid out a glittery, silver path across the water. A smudged magnet, it gently tugged the ocean back and forth against the shore. Overhead, he could spot Scorpio's glittering hooked tail and pincers in the sky.

The automatic was tucked into the waistline of his pants, hidden beneath the white short-sleeved shirt hanging outside his pants. *Just in case.* The gun wasn't loaded; he could fake out a knife-wielding junkie. If the junkie had a gun, he'd hand over the few dollars in his wallet. It was incredible how he had to plan these things out. In Havana, and in Miami, he had spent much time on the beach at night. He loved swimming under the stars. The ocean black and silver, the heavens the same, each reflecting upon the other—the continuum of continuums.

About five blocks down, he turned and trotted back to

the guesthouse.

As he was drinking cognac at the bar, Ana and Luis Concepción arrived. They greeted Bernardo warmly, as though this were a reunion of the long separated, rather than the usual weekly visit by the two who lived down the street. Between eight and nine in the mornings, Ana Concepción startled the neighborhood with pounding renditions of danzas, mambos and boogie-woogie on the grand piano in the front parlor of their house. Attorney Luis Concepción, silver-haired, in his mid-fifties, tall and erect, was dressed in a long-sleeved, white guayabera, dark pants and patent leather, black shoes. Ana, in her late forties, but looking ten years younger, was stylish and, Bernardo thought, still sensually appealing in a black, silk pants suit. Ana's eyes were large, soft and deep brown. At the bar, Bernardo retrieved two glass tumblers a n d poured them their usual Felipe Segundo brandies.

"We heard from Jorgito," said Ana. "He'll be home tomorrow. He said to tell tío Bernardo that he will have a surprise for him."

"The head of Fidel?" Bernardo smiled.

"We have a son who actually is helping that bastard's government meet its sugar quota," said Luis, grimacing.

"All right, Luis," said Ana, prepared to cut off a not unusual tirade from her husband about that *sinverguenza*

Castro and at times, his equally shameless son. "You know Jorgito is an idealist," said Ana. "He's always been a good son, for as long as he's been with us."

Luis shook his head, finished off his brandy, then asked Bernardo for another. "His political beliefs... I could never..." Luis' voice trailed off and he downed half of the next drink. Luis' jaw was set tight. He could still love his son, but it was often difficult knowing how ungrateful the boy—the young man who was now an instructor at the University— was.

Ana looked to Bernardo, who gave her a little nod and turned to Luis. "I asked Jorge, before he left, to bring us back a letter of apology. Fidel is stepping down and Cuba is holding free elections. All is forgiven. You and I have been invited back home."

"When Havana freezes over and all the *gusanos* go ice skating," said Luis winking, loosening up.

Bernardo and Luis touched palms. "That shouldn't be too long."

Ana moved to the end of the bar, where the 1950s-style countertop jukebox was attached to the wall. A Select-O-Matic that played 45 rpms, the jukebox came with Bernardo's purchase of the guesthouse. The songs were all oldies. Ana flipped through the metal-edged pages, then reached into her small, black-beaded purse and put quarters into the coin slot on the jukebox's top. She pressed letters and numbers in two tiled rows at the bottom and Nat "King" Cole began to sing, *"Aquellos Ojos Verdes."* Ana returned to where Luis was sitting and taking her husband's hand, gently coaxed him to dance in the small space between the bar and the tables. Tito Rodriguez followed with *"lnolvidable"* and Bernardo looked on approvingly as the couple danced a graceful bolero.

"Too much, too much," said Luis Concepción as he returned to the bar to finish his Felipe Segundo.

"Just enough," said his wife.

"You're wonderful dancers," said Bernardo.

"Almost thirty years of practice," said Luis. He looked with moderately drunk love at his wife. "She still excites me greatly. Here," he tapped his heart, "and, well, you know the other place."

"Ai, Luisito." She punched him lightly on the arm. *Abrazos* were exchanged all around and the couple left.

Back in Bernardo's room, the muffled crash of the waves were drowned out by the sound of cars racing along Ashford Avenue. The sound of the sea returned, then, the cars and more thoughts:

The cars zooming along Ocean Drive all hours of the night. The old Jews, sitting on beach chairs across from the traffic, wearing floppy hats. Morris playing his accordion, singing songs in Yiddish. The air-conditioning breaking down in the lobby of those rundown hotels and the front doors open to the revving motors and the car fumes and the moths that tick against the overhead lights and the flying roaches that wing in with soft thumps onto the front desk where Bernardo works as a night clerk-handyman. The creaking tiny elevators, getting stuck between floors. "Get Bernie! Where's Bernie?"

The large topographical map of Cuba, "borrowed" by Raft Santos from the local office of the U. S. Corps of Army Engineers, taped up on the wall in the back room of Manolo's restaurant, the best places for a landing circled in red. Mario Fonseca, the "Mr. Fix-it" lawyer—he knows the right judges —stands by the map, pointer in hand. Veteran of the Brigade 2506, repatriated to Miami after the Bay of Pigs disaster, he says: "We do it ourselves this time! That fucking Kennedy, pulling out our air cover, that cabrón, *he got what he deserved!"*

Bernardo and fifteen, twenty of his compatriotas *sit around tables in the back room, the ice cubes clinking as the rum and scotch are drained from glasses. The aroma of the Cuban earth hangs in blue clouds from the lit Montecristos and Sir Winstons smuggled in by relatives.*

"We are now giving serious consideration to the old CIA plan, the invasion taking place in the city of Trinidad, about 270 kilometers south-east of Havana...Foothills of the

Escambray...Sancti Spiratus province...Excellent port facilities, an easily defensible beachhead. If necessary, an escape through the mountains...guerilla tactics..."

¡Basta! thinks Bernardo. Enough! No more invasions, coups, juntas, revolutions. What he wants is involvement in things that expand, not shrink—the soul.

After the meeting, he decides it is only right to tell Licenciado Fonseca of his decision. This is his last meeting; they will have to find another builder and blower-up of bridges for the next landing. "My head, and my heart, are somewhere else," he tells Fonseca. He expects...He doesn't know what.

The lawyer stares long, hard, his jowls quivering, his eyelids slowly descending.

"¡Sucio traidor!"

He, Bernardo, is a filthy traitor. Loud and clear.

The room tenses in silence. The others, getting ready to leave, turn to the two men standing in front of the map of their homeland.

Bernardo's head goes light, the nerves tingle down his arms. He is half the lawyer's age, many inches taller and in much better shape from his racquet ball workouts. In his mind, he tears into the lawyer, smashing fists into his flabby body and obscenely drink-bloated face.

As Bernardo exits the room, most of his compatriotas

either peer at him with questioning wrinkled brows or look away.

After three years of Miami, he leaves for New York exiled from his fellow exiles.

When Bernardo awoke, his children had already left for school. It was past nine. A boulder seemed to rest on his soul. He pulled himself from bed and went to the bathroom, then twisted open the window's wooden louvers. Two long, black container ships appeared motionless on the sun-hazed horizon.

In the patio, Carmencita was serving bread, jam, papaya and coffee to a young couple staying in the guesthouse. He went into the kitchen and made himself *café Cubano* and spread butter and jam on some *pan de agua*. He carried his food and the newspapers back outside and greeted the tourist couple, who smiled back vacantly. He browsed the front pages, then flipped through the *San Juan Star.* An Associated Press story caught his eye.

LYONS WITNESSES IDENTIFY BARBIE IN ONE-DAY DEPORTATION O F 650

LYON, (AP) - Rolande Claire, a tall, slightly graying 63-year old woman from Lyons, kept a 43-year-old promise today. She stood before the court trying Klaus Barbie, the wartime Gestapo chief of Lyon, and recalled the events of Aug. 11, 1944, the day about 650 prisoners were assembled at Montluc prison here and sent to the concentration camps of Germany and Poland, where most of them died.

Mrs. Claire said that in the prison yard a Mrs. Gouttebelle—she did not give her first name—pointed out the Nazi officer to her who she said had tortured her and her husband.

"Look at him carefully and remember his name—Barbie," she quoted Mrs. Gouttebelle saying. "Promise me that if you survive and I don't come back, you will tell who he was, so that I will be avenged."

Mrs. Claire was among six witnesses..."

His mother's parents, three sisters, her two brothers, numerous aunts, uncles, cousins. The box cars, the camps, the crematoriums, up the chimneys, soot over the land. Only his mother and a sister escape. They were sent out two weeks before the Nazis rounded up the rest. Two more weeks in Poland, and he would never have been.

In his homeland, Juan Alvarez, Bernardo's father, a journalist and highly regarded literary critic, writes eloquently intemperate words about the future dictator and picks up his

Mauser to defend Madrid against the Franco fascists. Juan then chooses exile in France. In Paris, he meets a young teacher, Sophie Levi, an escapee from the Nazi occupation of Poland. When the Nazis march into the city, he and his young bride escape to the south of France, where they become a caretaker couple in the homes of the wealthy. In the city of Marseilles, Bernardo is born.

One of the couple's clients, a manufacturer of ships' parts who knows of their backgrounds, warns them of the impending roundup in Marseilles of Jews and other undesirables. The sympathetic M. Le Blanc helps smuggle Juan, Sophie, and two-year-old Bernardo aboard a neutral Irish cargo ship destined for the Caribbean.

Bernardo spent the afternoon on more repairs—faucets that needed new washers to stop leaking, more repainting; this time, of the flaking second-floor hallway ceiling. Later, he gave Anita permission to stay overnight at Patricia's house and he grilled hot dogs for Pablito. After dinner, he helped Pablito with his fifth-grade math homework. If Carlos had twenty-four marbles and he gave one-third of them to José and one-fourth to María, how many would he have left for himself? "Ten!" answered Pablito, arriving at the answer quicker than Bernardo.

After Pablito went to bed, Bernardo picked up *Anna Karenina* from the night stand next to his bed. He had to start the book, feeling guilty at his lack of a complete literary education. But just after Vronsky went to the train station to pick up his mother where got his first look at Anna and the "suppressed eagerness" in her face, Bernardo's mind left the station and he was carried into sleep's dark tunnel.

A small green-scaled lizard springs out of the palm of his hand and disappears in the Cruz de Malta bush outside his house. Papi has disappeared into the night and he asks Mami where he is. Tears roll down her burnished cheeks and she covers her mouth and holds Bernardo to the softness of her breasts; and then he is on the steps of the University, handing out leaflets against the dictator. He is in the streets cheering with Felipe, Joaquin and Quique as the barbudos drive by in their battered jeeps. "¡Viva Cuba libre!¡Viva Fidel!" Fellow engineer Joaquin Godoy issues stentorian snores from across the room as Bernardo slips out of his bed, throws on dark pants and a black shirt. He leaves the door open just slightly. Shutting it could wake his roommate. Carrying his shoes, he pads down the terrazzo floor to the end of the lobby; the window gives off on a dark alley two stories down. He creaks the window open and looks down. In the darkness, the drop looks considerable.

He puts one leg over the window sill, twists, turns, grabs the sill, lifts the other leg and turns his back to the darkness. He lowers his body slowly, moving his hand across until his fingers are on the outer edge of the window sill. He holds onto a metal edge by his fingertips and hangs there until the muscles in his arms and legs begin to ache. Then, he lets go.

He hears the crack, but feels nothing. When he tries to stand, his left foot curls in agonizing pain. He drops his shoes near a large garbage bin, half-limps, half-drags himself out of the cat-smelling alley.

The Paseo de la Reforma is lit up and still packed with zooming vehicles. The thin Mexico City air makes it difficult to breathe. He manages to stop a taxi to take him to the American Embassy that is several blocks down the avenue. Some lights shine from the upper floors of the embassy, yet he decides not to approach the Marines patrolling outside. He'll wait until morning when the regular staff gets to work.

He struggles to a spot under an aluminum awning across the street. Luckily, the night is mild. His ankle has turned blue and swells out like a baseball. Lying on several sheets of El Universal gathered from a trash can, he passes out from the pain. He comes to. He falls asleep, keeps waking.

At daybreak he finally sees people entering the embassy. He drags himself across the street. He tells the Marines at the door that he has been sent to Mexico by Fidel to an engineer's conference on building bridges. He wants to leave his country. The Marines help him inside and he applies for political asylum.

Fingers are wagged at him by both Americans and Cubans. He repeats as loud as he can shout with his shortened breath: "I want to leave!" A huge photo of Fidel scowls down at him from the wall. What is that photo doing in the American Embassy? He has made a terrible...

His foot is in a cast. He moves with crutches down Collins Avenue, Miami Beach. In the back room of the restaurant, he tells them: "Forget it, another invasion won't work." And they call him, "traidor," "cobarde" and the anger and guilt propel him around the room where he smashes his fist into faces. He believes he wakes, then believes he wills himself back to sleep, and sees himself at the entrance to the University again, dashing up and down across the wide steps, not wanting to miss out on any of his fellow students as he hands out the leaflets urging them to join the general strike called by the Llano. It's the first year the University has reopened after Batista shut it down two years before, and now the tyrant and his cruel government are gone. So, why is the urban underground calling a strike against Fidel? He believes in The Revolution. He believes in Fidel. So why is he, Bernardo, working against Fidel?

Don't question. History will absolve you.

The militia comes through the Greek columns at the top of the steps. The sun glints off the upturned hands of the bronze Alma Mater and a shot explodes in the air and a female student screams again and again.

He woke to screams coming from the alleyway...

Robert Friedman

Chapter 2

Sally was screaming blue murder as the guy took off toward the beach. "Help! Thief! Goddamn thief!" She collapsed against a wall, squatted and held a handkerchief below her left eye.

A tall, bare-chested fellow in khakis came running down the alley, bounding toward her. "Are you all right?"

"He stole my bag. I got everything in there. Just go after him and get it back!"

The fellow looked down at Sally whose face was crunched up in pain. "Let me just look…"

"Forget about it! Just go after him. It's all in the bag—my American Express checks, my plane ticket, my credit cards. That sonovabitch! Get my bag back and beat the bastard to a pulp! He's half your size. Get him! Go! Go!"

The fellow ran to the end of the alley and hoisted himself over a low wall and down onto the beach. After several minutes, he came back to where Sally waited, shaking his head. Sally groaned.

"I'll call the police," the tall guy said.

"Forget it. Maybe if I'm lucky somone'll find the bag after he dumps it and they'll return my empty wallet. The photos of Cheryl, my granddaughter, in the wallet, that's the only thing that's really important to me."

"Would you like to come into the guesthouse around the corner? I'm the owner. I have a first-aid kit there and you can use the telephone if you want. Or just rest up for a while."

Sally gave a curt nod. "Thanks."

The guesthouse owner introduced himself as Bernardo Alvarez.

"Sally," she said.

Bernardo helped Sally to her feet. She wobbled for a moment in her heels and held on to his arm as he led her around the corner toward the guesthouse. The electric lines above the street were sparking and crackling and Sally tightened her hold on the fellow's arm.

"Don't be frightened," he said. "That happens a lot here. It's the moisture in the air."

Sally nodded. "I thought that bastard was back and shooting at us."

As they entered the guesthouse, a young girl peered down from the staircase.

"Is everything all right, Papi? I heard screaming and I got

scared. You weren't in your room."

"Everything's okay, *mi amor.* There's nothing to worry about. Go back to bed." The young girl returned to her room.

Bernardo brought Sally to the couch inside his office. "That was my daughter," he said. "Let's have a look at your wound." Sally pulled the handkerchief away from under her eye.

He examined the torn skin beneath the already swollen, blackening eye. From the bottom drawer of his desk he pulled out a green plastic box and took out a gauze pad. "May I?"

Sally nodded. He gently dabbed the wound with the alcohol pad. Sally caught her breath; he carefully dabbed antibiotic cream around the bruising and covered it with a Band-Aid. "There. It doesn't look too bad. Do you want to make a telephone call?"

"Nah, there's no one to call. This is my last night here. I already checked out of my hotel and checked my luggage at the airport. My plane leaves real early, at seven. Of course, now I don't have my goddamn ticket..."

"Maybe if you call the airline and explain..."

"Yeah, I'll do that," said Sally. "But just let me sit here for a moment and collect my thoughts. Jeez, something told me I shouldn't have trusted that sonovabitch. I was just going for a last one before taking a taxi to the airport where I was going to nap for a couple of hours before my plane took off, then I planned to sleep on the plane. One night less to pay at the Hilton, save a couple of hundred bucks after I pissed so much away in the casino, y'know?"

Bernardo nodded.

"So I'm in the lounge, getting a last one before they close and this guy, Hector something-or-other—probably wasn't his real name anyway—I think he was following me and hanging around the casino while I was there. He comes up to me, a good-looking kid with slick black hair, and starts talking. So I'm just being polite, and when the lounge closes he asks if I want to go to an all-night club. Since I'm gonna be up all night anyway, I say okay. What a dumbbell!

"So he gets a taxi to take us, he says, to the club, only the cab leaves us at the corner here and he says the club is right down the street, and then he pulls me down the alley and I think here comes the rape. But instead he starts to pull my bag off my shoulder and while we're fightin' over it, he punches me in the eye and grabs the bag and takes off while I'm screamin' for help."

Bernardo kept nodding.

"Listen," Sally said, "you're really a swell guy, helping me like this. Look, my hands, they're still shaking. You wouldn't happen to have some liquor around to calm me down before I take off?"

Bernardo went back to the bottom desk drawer and

pulled out a bottle of Rémy Martin. "Is this okay?" he asked, holding it up so she could see its label.

"Sure. That's fine."

"I'll be right back."

Bernardo left the office. Sally caught a look at herself in the tile-framed mirror on the wall across from the couch. At least her Madonna pendant was still hanging around her neck. The bastard didn't yank that off.

She scratched one of her deeply tanned arms beneath her sleeveless, yellow blouse, which she pushed down tighter into the waistline of her Jordache jeans. *The gray is spreading into the blonde. She's gonna need a new dye job.*

She pushed back the loose strands of hair that fell over her ears. Her damn comb was in her bag! Creases were breaking through her makeup. *A sweaty, middle-aged, been through-it-all face. Okay, but not unattractive. What the hell.*

A moment later, Bernardo came back holding two brandy glasses by their stems. He poured a generous amount of the Rémy Martin into the two glasses and handed one to Sally.

"Thanks. You're a gentleman."

Sally looked deep into the glass, swirled the red-brown cognac around, took a sip, and then shot down the rest. She let out a deep sigh of relief. She eyed the bottle, then

Bernardo.

"Another one?"

"Just one more. I had rheumatic fever when I was a kid and the few I have each day keep the old heart ticking. This is really good brandy. You are indeed a gentleman."

Bernardo poured Sally another drink.

"Geez, what a jerk I was to trust that S. O. B," Sally said. "I'm always getting into situations with creeps, present company of course not included. Sally the Sucker."

She drank half the glass of cognac, then continued. "I guess he reminded me of Joe, when he was goin' out with me before we got married; the same long black hair and the chin always sticking out, like he was daring someone to hit him, but with that glint in his eye saying if anyone did, they sure would be sorry. Joe's a labor organizer and he's got friends that'll lie down in front of a truck for him. When Toni, she's my daughter, got married, Joe got a hall in Astoria for the wedding through his union connections. We got it for a song. So I tell this…this Hector, about Joe because I didn't want him coming on to me, you know? And Hector swears he's a loyal member of the Teamsters and leads strikes in Puerto Rico, blah, blah, blah…he's so full of shit."

Sally drank. She looked at Bernardo. He nodded. She poured herself another.

"You want to call the airline now?" Bernardo asked.

"Yeah, I guess I should."

Bernardo picked up the phone that rested on top of a telephone directory on the desk and pulled the directory to him. "I'll get the number for you. What airline are you traveling on?"

"Eastern. No, wait, I changed it to American. No, I changed it to Eastern. Damn, who remembers?"

Bernardo wrote down the numbers of both airlines. He was about to hand the phone to Sally, but she was busy downing more Rémy. He dialed the phone numbers and got recordings giving him 800 numbers that referred him back to the closed local offices.

"I guess you'll have to go directly out to the airport and explain what happened."

"Yeah, that's the best thing to do. I still have some time. Where was I? Yeah, so Toni, my baby? She gets pregnant and we go to the family—lovely people from Napoli, but very nice —and the father beats the son to a pulp and we arrange this wedding. It was a beautiful affair. And she had Cheryl, that doll. That bastard sonovabitch stole the photos of my granddaughter!

"So the marriage lasted less than a year. Toni would come home with bruises all over. I'd ask her what happened and she'd say, 'nothin', Ma. I fell,' or she was in a taxi that got hit by another car or a door slammed on her fingers. Then one night, she comes in with *two* black eyes. She looks like Andy Panda and I told her, 'Don't tell me a door did that. ' And she broke down and told me how that guinea was always beating her. Joe heard about it and he got so angry he went over there and made Toni pack up and come home and waited for him to come home from work—a job in the office of a construction company. Joe got it for him. And he was going to kill that bastard till I pleaded with him. We went to his parents and his father beat him to a pulp again and…"

"Why don't you rest for a while?" Bernardo said. "You can have a room…"

Sally nodded, then went on. "And me, I told you about me and Joe? See what I'm wearing around my neck? Joe and I visited the Vatican in Rome just after we got married and he bought this for me there. The Madonna is ivory. A couple of the pearls dropped off around the sides which I'm gonna have to have them replaced, but I always wear it, for luck or something. One of the few days I wasn't wearing it, the 'accident' happened. Some accident. The sonsovbitches; his own union, for chrissake! They did it to him. Well, some of the guys there, they didn't like the way Joe was running the local, so they did something to his car. And it was a rainy night and the brakes didn't work. And it was right when he was getting off the BQE, the Brooklyn-Queens Expressway, just a couple of blocks off it leads to our house. He crashed into the back of that trailer truck and he's been in a wheelchair now for six years. At least the union is taking care of him with the health insurance and the checks, but, now he's…we don't… Jesus Christ!"

She broke down as the tears flowed and her shoulders shook. Bernardo got up and put a hand on Sally's shoulder. She grabbed his hand with both of hers and squeezed it. "Jesus Christ."

"I think you should rest awhile," Bernardo said, pulling his hand away from hers. "You can have the room right across from the office. I'll put an alarm clock in the room and set it for five-thirty, which will give you a couple of hours of sleep. You can call for a taxi. I'll leave the number next to the telephone here, then, hopefully you can get things squared away at the airport. I'll lend you some money. You can pay me back when you get home."

"Yeah, thanks. Jeez." She looked around in a vain search for her bag, then remembered it was stolen and asked Bernardo if he had a Kleenex. He gave her his handkerchief and she wiped the running tears and mascara and blew her nose. "I'm sorry," she said, looking down at the handkerchief. "I'll wash it out for you."

"It's okay, keep it. Just one minute."

Bernardo went behind the front desk outside the office, took a key from one of the room slots and opened the door to the room across from the desk. He turned down the covers on the bed, turned on the air-conditioning and switched on the lights and the ceiling fan. The air-conditioning groaned and sputtered, then kicked in. He went back out to a closet in the hallway, got some towels and brought them back to the room.

He went upstairs to his room, got a travel alarm clock and took three twenties out of his wallet. He put the money in an envelope with the guesthouse's return address stamped in the corner, wrote the phone numbers of two taxi services on the envelope, pocketed the clock and the envelope, then returned to his office. Sally was sunken into a corner of the couch with her head on her chest, her face crunched up, her legs on the floor, and snoring. Bernardo shook her lightly by the shoulder. Her eyes shot open and she stared questioningly at him. Then she smiled and closed her eyes again.

Bernardo bent down at the waist beside her, tucked his arms under her legs and lifted her from the couch. He carried her into the room he had prepared for her and lay her on the bed, then put a sheet over her. Her eyes still shut, she smiled and said, "Thanks, Joe. It don't matter. I still love you."

Sally slept till noon. She rushed from her room, disheveled. No one was behind the front desk and the door to the office was closed. She went to the patio. Bernardo was cleaning out glasses behind the bar. She began yelling at him for not waking her.

"How am I supposed to get on the plane now? It's already in New York. I can't believe this!"

"I set the alarm for five-thirty. You overslept six hours," said Bernardo, angered at her anger.

"Yeah, well...Jesus!"

Sally frowned and shook her head, as though Bernardo, all men, the human race would never learn how to treat her. Then she said, "You got any coffee around here?"

"Sit at a table," Bernardo said. "I'll get you a cup."

He served her coffee, not with a smile.

Bernardo said he would call a taxi for her; he went to his office. After a couple of minutes, a cabbie blew his horn from the street.

Now Sally was all guilty smiles. "Hey, I'm sorry. I'm really a nasty bitch when I wake up. Thanks for everything. You're a true gentleman. I'll send you the money as soon as I get home. I appreciate your help. I really do."

"Okay," answered Bernardo.

Bernardo helped Sally out of the house and into the taxi, gave the driver a twenty and told him to take her to the airport. Sally waved from the back seat window. Bernardo's smile shook as he waved back. She saw him shaking his head as he went back to the guesthouse.

At six the evening, Sally returned.

She made her re-entrance accompanied by a short, broad-shouldered guy with a pock-marked, tough-looking face. He was carrying Sally's two large suitcases.

"Would you believe I couldn't get on another flight today?" Sally told Bernardo, who was nursing a beer at the bar. She parked herself on a stool. Her companion looked around, then put the suitcases by the soda machine.

"You wouldn't *believe* what I had to go through to convince those people who I was before I got everything ripped off. I even showed them the tag on my luggage with my name and address on it, but they wanted to know why I didn't report what happened to the cops. I told them none of their frigging business why. So, anyway, they said all the flights were booked and they'd 'process' a new ticket and they'd call me as soon as it came through. I hope you don't mind; I gave the guesthouse here as where I'm stayin'. You think I could have that room where I was last night for another night?"

Bernardo nodded. He gave a forced smile. "It's all right."

"Gee, thanks a million." Sally turned to her companion with a bright smile. "I told you he was a real stand-up guy."

Then, still looking at her companion, she told Bernardo: "This is Pete Sánchez, the chief of the Teamsters here. He's an old friend of Joe's, who I called this morning and he called Pete who kindly picked me up at the airport and offered to buy another ticket for me but all the airlines were booked. Anyway, Pete also knows some people who he thinks will be able to contact that 'Hector' from last night. They're gonna convince him to return my purse and everything that was in it."

"A pleasure to meet you," said Pete Sánchez, shaking Bernardo's hand.

"The same."

"Time for my medicine," Sally said with a wide grin. She asked the bartender for a double scotch. Sánchez had a DonQ on the rocks.

Perry, the bartender, told the union leader he had been following his "exploits" in the press.

"He tried to frame me," said Sánchez.

Perry gave his purse-lipped, sympathetic bartender's nod. "That's the feds for you," he said.

"The same old shit," Sánchez said. "Blame the Teamsters. I never met that asshole who leads the hotel-restaurant union down here. The sonovabitch was trying to organize our guys in the hotels which we got to first. The fucker probably got beat up by his own guys. So what happens? They bring us to court; me and three of my guys. They get convicted. I was in Las Vegas at the time, so they had to let me go. How could I take part in the supposed kidnapping and beating?"

Everyone drank. Sánchez ordered another round. The union leader noticed the tattoo on Perry's left arm, the *Semper Fi* on the blue ribbon in the U. S. flag-covered eagle's mouth.

"Jarhead? Nam?"

"Beirut," Perry said with a sad smile.

Sánchez bit his lip and shook his head. He pulled up a trouser leg and pushed down his sock to show Perry lumpy scar tissue slathered from the side of his knee down to his ankle. "Khe Sanh, Third Marines. At least we were at war."

"Yeah," said Perry. "You met the enemy, and it wasn't you." Sánchez hooded his eyes. He frowned. "Un-huh."

A new arrival at the bar said: "Something ice cold, please. A ginger ale or a Coke. No, not a Coke. Those sonsovbitches fix it so that new soft drink patents are kept off the market."

The guy bobbed his narrow head on his long, thin neck toward Bernardo, Sally and Sánchez . On top of his forehead was a clump of reddish brown hair. His eyes, behind thick glasses, darted from side to side. He looked like a near-sighted, paranoid giraffe. He clutched a faded thick, pink accordion folder to his chest as though it were a crucial body appendage. He wore a dark jacket that may have once fitted his extra-scrawny frame, a yellowed white shirt and a sixties flower-power tie of bursting yellows, reds and purples. He took off his horn-rimmed glasses and wiped them with his tie. His long, pale, bony face was damp, as though it had just been sprayed. He shook sweat out of an ear, then took deep gulps from the tall glass of ginger ale, his Adam's apple bobbing with the intake.

"Jeez, first I'm freezing in that damn courthouse for three hours, then I'm boiling waiting for the bus which wasn't even going to the Condado. I had to get off before the bridge and walk the rest of the way. No wonder I'm always getting a cold." On cue, his nose exploded in a series of sneezes. He wiped it with something raggedy and gray that he took from a back pocket.

Sally made a face.

Speaking to everyone and no one in particular, the guy said: "Okay, I was back in Figueroa's courtroom for a change, one more hearing. You'd think, on second thought, which he always has since he's always sounding off, saying things that have absolutely *no* bearing on what's going on, *obiter dictum,* if you know what I mean, you'd think he would finally give me my day in court. But this time he pulls us into his chambers, the lawyers for General Motors and me. In all modesty, although I don't have their fancy diplomas from Harvard or Yale, I could run rings around these high-priced shysters in any courtroom, whether it's in Puerto Rico or Peoria. I forgot more about this case, which is almost nothing, than these fabulous fakes will ever know about it. So, anyway, Figueroa says he got the writ of *certiorari* from the Boston Appeals Court, which I'm going to because of his stupid ruling last month that the *onus probandi* falls on me. You know I didn't show, according to him, *de facto,* how those thieves stole *my* design, even though anyone who reads the papers on file with half a brain, which Figueroa evidently lacks, can understand my complaint *prima facie.* And if the gangsters at GM had half a conscience they would plead *nolo contendere,* even though I would still sue because these crooks have cost me millions of dollars."

He drained the liquid left in his glass, then bit down on the ice cubes like they were pieces of hard candy. He took a deep breath, looked around, then stared at Sally's escort. "Hey! I know you!"—he pointed a quivering finger at the union leader—"you're the guy who beat the government, right? You beat the feds in their own court! How d'ya do it?"

Pete Sánchez rehooded his eyes and stared at the tip of the guy's dripping nose.

"Sorry." The guy extracted the rag again, wiped and blew. "I sat in on some of the trial. How did you beat 'em?"

"I was innocent. They framed me," said Sánchez. "They never proved—"

"Yeah, but how did you *beat* them? The judge was Acevedo, right? I hear he's expensive as hell. Did they pay from union headquarters?"

"What the hell are you talking about?"

"Come *on*. We all know what it takes to get an acquittal from the feds in this court here."

Sánchez looked at the guy, contemplating how to pulverize him. He decided to turn his back and ignore the asshole, who shrugged, then smiled at Sally, who also turned away.

"Well, I guess I'll be going. I got another writ to write up," he said and left.

"Jeez, what a creep!" said Sally.

"A jerk-off," said Sánchez.

"That's Burt Cherry. He's a monomaniac," Perry said. "He gets one thing in his head, he can't get rid of it. It warps his whole life."

Sánchez gave Perry a reassessing look, as though letting him know that was no way for an ex-Marine to deduce —an asshole was an asshole.

After a couple of more rounds of drinks, Bernardo announced it was time to close the bar. "We close up early one night a week," he told Sally.

Sally looked offended, as though the move were being made because of her and her guest. "Okay," she said. "There were lots of other bars in town."

The next day, Sally told Bernardo she had decided to

accept Pete Sánchez's offer to fill in as his assistant while his regular secretary went on an emergency vacation for a week. She had to take care of a sick sister who recently lost her husband.

"I told Joe and he's all for it. I'd love to continue staying at the guesthouse here if it's all right. Pete gave me an advance last night so I can pay you for the room right now, plus what I owe you."

Sally dug into a new leather over-the-shoulder bag for her new wallet, from which she began to pull out crisp twenty-dollar bills.

"You don't have to pay right away." "No, no, I wanna pay now, and give you a week's rent—while I still have it."

They settled up, passing money between them. "Thanks again for everything," Sally said. "If you need me to do anything..."

"That's all-right," Bernardo said. He started to turn and Sally saw him biting down on his lower lip.

The next night at half an hour before midnight, "Hector," who had ripped off Sally, appeared at the Solimar Guesthouse. He was accompanied by two *"companieros"*—a six-foot-four guy with neck, shoulders and arms like ham hocks and a foot-shorter version with similar steroid-inflated muscles. They wore dark sunglasses, black T-shirts and tense facial expressions.

Bernardo was stacking beach chairs scattered around the patio and Sally was at the bar sipping a double scotch. The three men approached the bar through the still-open beach gate. Hector, also wearing dark sunglasses, was steered, then pushed toward Sally. He had a large patch of taped gauze across his forehead. His guides stood off to the side.

"Hello, *mi amor,*" Hector said.

Sally, who had been regaling Perry with the sad stories of her family's lives, did a double-take. *"Sonovabitch!"* she screamed.

"Hey, cool it," Hector said, forcing a smile. He grimaced. All parts of his body, including his face muscles, appeared to be hurting. "I come by to return stuff to you that I admit I stole, but realize now that I never should have hit on you. So I want to apologize and return this to you." He dug into both his pants pockets and put several things on the bar in front of Sally: her wallet, a snapped-together black folder of American Express checks, an Eastern Air Lines ticket folder, two sets of keys, a rabbit's foot, a box of Marlboros, and a pack of Life Savers.

"I'm sorry but I threw away your bag and some of the other stuff in it, like perfume and toothbrushes and some other crap," Hector said. "All your money is in the wallet, every cent."

He threw a look to the guys standing off to the side. Their expressions did not change.

Sally stared hard at Hector. "What a piece of shit you are," she said.

"Hey I returned everything. I apologized. What else you want?" Hector turned to his two escorts. "Okay? I did it all, right? I apologized. She got everything back."

He started toward the gate leading to the beach. The other two followed. Then, just before reaching the gate, Hector's legs wobbled and dipped and he shuffled forward, then back, as though doing an awkward mambo. He reached out to grab the gate in front of him, then grabbed at his chest and collapsed in a heap.

The escorts looked at one another and the shorter man nodded toward the gate. They stepped around Hector and took off down the beach.

Bernardo, watching this take place, approached and turned Hector on his back. Hector was wheezing. "C-can't breathe. Ch-chest hurts." He broke into a steady, strangulating cough.

Sally called over from her bar stool, "Is he dying, I hope?"

Bernardo squatted down and took off Hector's sunglasses. Both eyes were blackened. "He doesn't look too good."

"That breaks my heart," Sally said.

Hector's wheezing got deeper and his coughing continued. He grasped his chest and began groaning.

Bernardo told Perry, "You better call for an ambulance."

Perry came out from behind the bar and went to the front desk to make the call. Sally slipped off the barstool and stood over Hector. He had a frightened look in his blackened eyes. He closed his eyes, "I ca-can't br-breathe good. Oh-h-h-h."

Sally kept staring down at Hector. He opened his eyes and looked up. "I apologized," Hector reminded her.

"Yeah," she said.

"My chest hurts!"

"As soon as the ambulance comes, they'll give you emergency help," Sally said. Hector nodded. He kept his eyes shut and reached up for her hand. She put both hands behind her back, shook her head, looked at Bernardo and made a face.

Perry came back. "I called 911 about ten times, and I got busy signals and a couple of recorded messages that the number was no longer in service, then busy signals again."

"I'll take him to the hospital in my car," Bernardo said. He turned to Hector. "We're going to get you up and take you to the hospital, okay?"

"Yeah. Okay."

Perry and Bernardo lifted Hector under his arms and carried him across the patio. Sally went to open the front door. Hector was deposited on the front steps while Bernardo went to get his car. Gasping for breath, Hector squeezed his arms across his chest.

Bernardo pulled the car along the curb. Perry picked Hector up under the arms again and deposited him into the back seat. Hector groaned. "I think I'm gettin' a heart attack."

Sally looked in the back seat. Hector, crunched up in a corner, made a feeble hand signal. "Come wit' me. Please."

Sally looked at Bernardo who shrugged.

"Please!" Hector's chin was trembling.

"Goddamn!" She got in the back seat.

Sally the sucker.

"I'll hang around until you get back," Perry told Bernardo.

They drove off across the city. It was Saturday night and the roads were crowded. Each time Bernardo braked Hector let out another groan. He took hold of Sally's hand and kept squeezing it.

Finally, they arrived at the government medical center.

The emergency room was packed and in barely-controlled chaos. They were told that there had been a shootout between drug gangs at a nearby housing project. Victims were being carried on stretchers, rolled in wheelchairs and staggering in on their own. People were rushing back and forth, imploring nurses and interns for one thing or another. Bernardo and Sally brought in Hector and lowered him into a chair. Music was blaring from a TV where dancers were gyrating to a meringue, the wounded were groaning and a crowd was packed around the admitting desk.

Sally's eyes were darting back and forth at the scene. "I can't *believe* this! This is *really* crazy! Let's get outta here."

"I thought the government hospital would take him right away since it's the largest on the island," Bernardo said. "Okay, we'll get him to a private hospital."

Hector was rocking back and forth in his chair and Bernardo shouldered him back onto his feet. A heavily wheezing Hector exclaimed, "What the *fuck?"*

"There's too much triage going on here," Bernardo said. "You'll have to wait hours before they get around to you."

Sally put her shoulder under Hector's other arm and they directed him to the car, which, luckily, was parked right outside.

It was past one a. m., and the Saturday night revelers still beeped, skidded and skirted around one another, causing jams along the highway and down the avenues.

They came off the highway and cut across town to another hospital, in the affluent Condado tourist area.

They drove up to Emergency and Bernardo put the car in park and got out. A stray wheelchair sat by the door. Bernardo rolled it up to the car and helped Hector into it.

"Take him inside while I park the car," he told Sally.

Sally wheeled Hector through automatic doors to the admitting desk. Hector's eyes were closed and he was gasping for air. The emergency room was filled, but there were no apparent gunshot victims. The triple-chinned woman behind the desk asked for the patient's ID. Hector reluctantly dug into his pocket and handed Sally his thin, beat-up wallet.

"I don't see a health insurance card," Sally said, looking through it. "There's no driver's license or credit card either."

His wallet held three cards. One of the cards advertised a strip nightclub. It had a phone number penciled on the back. A second offered a free doughnut with a second cup of coffee. The third was a Social Security card with his name and number.

"Let's see. His name...it ain't Hector. It's...*Je-sus!* His name is Jesus. Jesus Juan Calderon. Wow! He's a Jesus."

"I need an address," said the woman behind the admitting desk.

Bernardo came to the desk.

"There's none on the cards," Sally said. She asked Hector. "What's your address?"

He waved her off. "Get me a goddamn doctor!"

"Should I give the guesthouse as his address?" Sally asked Bernardo.

Bernardo frowned but nodded.

"Hey, I'm gettin' a heart attack," Hector-Jesus shouted. "I can feel it! Get me a doctor, please!"

Sally gave the guesthouse's address to the desk clerk. After she finished filling out the form, the desk clerk pressed a buzzer and two aides came out from the emergency ward with another wheelchair. They put Hector in the wheelchair carefully and the woman buzzed them back in to the ward.

Sally left the wallet on the admitting desk. "Let's get the hell out of here," she told Bernardo, turning to go.

"Sally. *¿Dónde está Sally?"*

Sally turned toward the voice and faced an orderly holding a clipboard.

"You Sally?"

Sally didn't answer.

The orderly cocked his head. Sally frowned, nodded.

"He wants you," said the orderly, looking down at the clipboard. "Heyzuz," the orderly said referring to Jesus. "He wants you."

"You got to be kidding."

The orderly shrugged. "He wants you," he repeated.

"Tell him to take…" Sally looked at Bernardo, who also

shrugged. "Oh, *Christ!"* She kept rubbing her chin, looking from Bernardo to the orderly, back to Bernardo.

"I'll wait for you here," Bernardo said.

"I'll just be a minute."

The orderly led Sally through the swinging doors to the emergency ward. The patients were lying in beds separated by curtains. In the center of the room, nurses and orderlies were working on charts, answering phone calls and calling for doctors through a speaker system. The orderly motioned Sally to the far end of the room. He pulled back a curtain. Jesus-Hector lay bare-chested on a bed, a male nurse bending over him attaching wired pads to different parts of his chest, his ankles and his wrists. The wires were attached to a machine on a table beside the bed. Numbers and lines flicked across green screens hanging from the wall above his head.

Hector spotted Sally at the foot of the bed. *"Mi amor.* Stay wit' me."

"Why?"

The nurse looked up at Sally and frowned.

"Because I need you to," Hector said.

"So?"

"Hey, I don't got nobody else," Hector said, as though that explained Sally's responsibility. He looked surprised that she didn't get it.

Sally dropped into a chair against the wall a few feet from the bed where Hector lay.

Sally the sucker.

"Hold still now," the nurse said. The machine on the table started making wavy lines on a long strip of paper. The nurse tore off the paper, hit something under the bed that propped Hector up halfway and told him, "The doctor will be here very soon."

"What did the machine say?" asked a worried Hector.

"The doctor will tell you," the nurse said, pulling open the front curtain, exiting, then closing the curtain from the outside.

Hector patted the side of the bed near Sally. "Please, hold my hand," he tried again.

Sally stared through Hector. "You want some pity from me? You should have thought of that before grabbing my bag and punching me in the eye."

"Hey, I told you how sorry I am and I mean that with all my heart. I had too many drinks before and then wit' you and when I drink like that I do stupid, crazy things I never would do otherwise. I been told by a doctor I got a sort of temporary insanity in my head. I can't help myself. Listen, we're all *en la lucha,* in the struggle, you know? Ask around, you'll find I'm really a great guy when I'm sober. I'm really sorry I hit you, but look how you bit my arm that made me do it."

Hector tore a bandage off his upper arm. The skin was red, somewhat raw and bumpy.

"So," he said. "All I'm askin' is that you give me a break."

Sally put the bandage back on Hector's arm. She sighed deeply. "I'm going real soon," she said.

"My kid."

"What?"

"I got a kid. I love that kid. I'd *die* for him. I can't trust who's supposed to be watching him 'cause she's a junkie. Just like the kid's mama. Lots of times she leaves before I get home. I just hope he's okay. I need to check up on him."

Jesus H. Christ!

They looked deep into each other's eyes. Hector flinched, Sally made a trembly sound as she let air out through her lips. Then she said: "I'm gonna be right back."

"Wha...?"

She opened and closed the curtain-door, walked around the crowded room of nurses and computers and out the swinging emergency room doors.

"Listen," she told Bernardo. "Why don't you go back to the guesthouse? I'm gonna wait with him for the doctor and see what's next. He's got a goddamn kid at home. We're not too far from your place and I'll catch a taxi."

Bernardo looked up quizzically, as though expecting further explanation.

"It's okay," she said. "I'll stick around."

"You sure?"

"Yeah. What the hell."

Sally went back through the swinging doors.

When the doctor finally arrived to examine Hector, the doctor said the electrocardiogram showed no blockage, no arrhythmia, no cardiomyopathy, no pericarditis, no myocardial infarction—in other words, the patient's heart seemed fine. After a few questions, Hector said he had asthma as a kid, but thought it was gone. The doctor wrote out a prescription in case he got short of breath again and released him. They called a taxi; Hector took Sally's arm going outside for the cab.

Luckily, there was an all-night pharmacy across the street from where Hector lived. Sally would fill the prescription, then get the hell out of there. But first she helped Hector up the four flights through the smelly hallway to his messy room on the top floor of the cruddy building where he lived. Across from a messy bed was a crib. Inside the crib sat a little boy. When he saw Hector and Sally he stood, grasped the bars on the side of the crib and let out long, loud wounded cries.

"Aw, Christ! That junkie downstairs was supposed to

put him asleep. She left the kid again so she could go get her goddamn fix!"

"Okay kid. Okay, okay," Hector said as he went to the small refrigerator in his tiny kitchenette and took out a bottle. "Here you go, my little man."

Hector gave the kid the bottle. The kid took it in his two hands and plopped down again in the crib and sucked greedily on it. Then he tossed the bottle into a corner and started crying again. Hector stumbled toward his bed. "Oh, man. I feel like shit." He collapsed on the bed. The kid was wailing.

Sally went to the crib and picked up the little boy. "Hey, sweetie. It's okay."

She cradled the tot, who stopped crying. His little toes wiggled and he smiled. His little face crinkled up. He began to play with the pendant around her neck. He was going to take it in his mouth but Sally pulled it away and fed him the bottle again. She smoothed the little curls on his head—like old times. The tot closed his eyes, still sucking, crunched up his face, stopped sucking, and started crying again. She laid him down in the crib.

"Where's the diapers?"

"I don't know. I think I brought them downstairs to the bitch who was watching him."

Jesus H. Christ!

Sally found the bathroom and went in it. At least, there was toilet paper. She brought the roll back to the crib and cleaned the kid. "Just hang in there, baby." The kid started crying again. "I'll be right back."

She left the apartment to fill the prescription and get a box of diapers.

Hector barely made it out of bed and back after she rung the bell. He was asleep again in record time and by then, the kid was also sleeping. Sally put the prescription drugs she paid fifty bucks for on the messy table in the center of the smelly room, diapered the kid, then, sat for a minute in an unraveling straw rocker.

When she woke, smudgy gray light was filtering through the one small, streaked window. She rose out of the rocker and made sure the baby looked okay, turning it from its stomach onto its back. The kid made a little noise, sighed. She stroked him softly on his chest, then left.

She walked fifteen minutes toward who the hell knows where before she caught a cab. She couldn't remember the name of the guesthouse but knew it was in the Ocean Park section of the city. The cab driver drove up and down the streets until she spotted the place, the Solimar Guesthouse. After paying the cab driver, she rang the guesthouse's bell, banged on the door, rang and banged. The door was finally opened by Carmencita, the cleaning woman.

Sally grunted and went to her room and collapsed on her bed. She should have just told that Hector creep to drop dead, after what he did to her. He deserved nothing better. Even with that poor little kid. Yeah, yet...

She thought of Toni and she thought of Cheryl. She thought of Joe, how in those early years she was able to melt that tough guy in her arms, between her legs. How, just after the accident, they even became closer just by holding each other. She fingered the pendant.

Then, in these last years she was always making excuses to go here and there, trips to South Jersey, to the Caribbean, with so-called friends or on her own. So instead of being home right now taking care of Joe, here she was stuck with El Creepo.

Yeah yet...what? If she had just left after he told her about the kid, what kind of bitch would she have been? She would check on Hector later; make sure the jerk was taking his medicine and that someone was taking care of the kid. She remembered the little toes, the crinkly smile and her heart melted.

The kid.

Joe.

Even that jerk, Hector.

Everybody was hurtin'.

The tears flowed.

Sally the Sucker.

Yeah, right.

Robert Friedman

Chapter 3

Burt Cherry returned after a McMuffin and coffee breakfast down the block. He looked around his room and boy, was he pissed! He had them on his bed organized by year, court, judge. Now they were stacked. . . who the hell knew how? He ran out to the lobby looking for Bernardo and ran into Carmencita, the cleaning woman. It would be useless telling her.

"Where's Bernardo? Where's that guy?"

Carmencita scrunched up her nose.

"Bernardo, the owner. *¿Dónde está?* Where the hell is he?"

Carmencita motioned her fuzzy head toward the patio, then put up a hand and went to get him. Burt waited at the front desk. *Can't anyone in this place do what he asks?*

A few moments later, Bernardo came toward him with a set smile on his face.

"Good morning, Mr. Cherry. How can I help you

today?"

"I told her not to, but she did it again!" Burt's gray eyes watered behind his glasses. He put one skinny, trembling arm on the front desk.

"The room. She moved everything in there. How many times have I told her not to do that?"

"But she tries to keep everything in place when she cleans up. She tells me she does."

Bert looked out through the open patio door at Carmencita who was washing down the tables. She was singing, "Stop, in the Name of Love" in a bell-clear, lilting voice, sounding amazingly like Diana Ross.

"Perhaps out of place were one or two papers..." Bernardo said.

"Come on! Not one or two. More than that, for Chrissake! You know how important these papers are to me. My case, for Chrissake. I was cheated out of a fortune by those miserable bastards! Come on, *you* know that." Burt looked hurt, as though Bernardo had forgotten.

Bernardo nodded.

"I don't want my papers disturbed. Have a heart for Chrissake!"

"If she doesn't straighten up the room, you complain. Yet, you won't put the papers on the table. They're often found on the bed and on the floor. If you want I'll put in a larger..."

Burt slowly shook his head. "Come on, come *on!* I have to sleep with my documents close by me. I have my whole goddamn life in those papers!" He took a deep breath, realizing he would have to explain again what should have been obvious.

"Look, in the year 1952, at the tender age of ten, I designed the sports car that was to become an all-time bestseller. I was a boy genius, *everyone* knew that. My car featured six 235. 5 cubic inch OHV, 'Blue Flame' aluminum pistons. I designed a fiberglass body before anyone else. That baby would ride on a modified X-frame chassis with a live axle suspended on elliptic springs. I drew it all up using warm gray crayon pencils on eight-and-a-half-by-eleven cover stock weight paper. Structurally, and every other goddamn way, it was a thing of beauty. Then those bastards at General Motors stole the design! Mass produced it and called it the Chevy Corvette. They made millions and I got *nada, nichts, rien de tout. Bubkis.* How do you think I've been feeling all these years?

"So I sued. Like you, or the whole goddamn world, don't know. I been in and out of the courts for the last twenty years. It was all set to go up to the Supreme Court in the early years, until Fortas the Fixer threw it out. They got to him, of course, gave him a heavy stock investment. *Everybody* knows that. Why do you think they kicked ol' Dishonest Abe off the bench? I am my case, my case is me. I have to keep bodily contact with my papers as much as possible, certainly during the nights. They could send in thieves while I sleep, take them off the table easily. They would do that. They're General Motors, the assholes of the automotive industry. As it is now, I'm taking a chance, I can carry only so many documents with me in my portfolio, but I have to file another writ of certiorari today. It's now 1987 and I'm *still* in court. You see why I need your cooperation? You get it now, right?"

Burt lifted his broomstick arm from the desk and extended it to Bernardo in a plea for understanding.

"All right, Mr. Cherry," Bernardo nodded. "I'll make sure Carmencita is very careful when she makes up your bed and cleans your room this morning."

Burt squinted his watery eyes and looked hard at Bernardo, as though bringing him into focus for the first time. Then he nodded. "Thanks. You're a good guy." He offered his hand to Bernardo. They shook hands and Burt went to the front door. As he stepped outside, he blinked and threw his free arm up over his eyes, as though the sun's sudden glare were exploding flashbulbs from paparazzi waiting for him out there. He switched his thick black-rimmed glasses for the aviator-style prescription sunglasses in his shirt pocket.

He crossed to McCleary, then down Loiza Street to the Baldorioty de Castro overpass, onto De Diego, to Ponce de Leon, then Fernandez Juncos Avenue, with the sun whacking the thinning spot on top of his head. It was one hell of a walk to get a damn bus going into Old San Juan. If he had waited for one on Loiza Street he'd be there forever. Already he was sweating like mad under his short-sleeved white shirt, down his rumpled gray slacks and into his black socks and scuffed brown loafers. His nose was dripping. He wiped and blew it in the raggedy hanky he took from his back pocket. The bottom of the portfolio he carried was soaked dark brown from his sweaty hand.

Here too, he waited, and waited, for a bus. A Number One going to the Old City finally arrived. The air-conditioning felt good. He got a seat in the back and opened the bow knot on his portfolio and took out the brief he typed up last night on his beloved Olivetti Lettera 2 2. He would file the brief as an addendum to his appeal of the summary judgment dismissing his motion to get those thieves at General Motors back in court. He held the sheet and reread the motion. His argument was undeniable—except to the crooked judges of the San Juan Federal Court, who must, he reasoned, be getting big payoffs from GM. He was asking for a hearing to reconsider the latest dismissal of his case, at which he knew he could run circles around the opposing lawyers. How could he be denied his day (all right, maybe his twentieth or thirtieth day) in court? Figueroa seemed a little better than the others who had heard his case. He at least made believe that he was giving Mr. Burt Cherry his day, or days, in court. Yeah, thought Burt, probably so that he could exhort more money from the GM shysters before dismissing the latest motion.

The bus rumbled along the ocean road leading into Old San Juan, passing low, tile-roofed buildings, minaret-like towers and ragged leaved palms, all wrapped in sun haze and sea mist; like a scene out of North Africa or the Mideast. But at least there were no Arabs around. Puerto Ricans were pains in the ass enough, imagine having to deal with Arabs!

Then came the National Guard armory, the local Legislature, looking just like the U. S. Capitol, the Carnegie Library, the YMCA—all signs of the good old U. S. takeover. Your average American was no bargain either, at least in the everyday dealings department. But at least they spoke the same language and had lots of the same feelings about things. That was b.s., too. The values and ideas of Americans were as screwed up as those of any other. Burt found this out growing up in Brooklyn and moving to Los Angeles before coming here.

He knew that he, himself, was sort of creepy. He had had it drummed in most of his 45 years by so-called friends at school, by the few girls he tried to date, by the guys in his company at Fort Leonard Wood before he got his medical discharge for "a nervous condition," and by relatives—other than his dad, who died when he was three, and his mom, who hugged him once in a while when she wasn't at work in department stores in downtown Brooklyn or attending her union meetings or out on dates with commie worker boyfriends listening to folk music in the Village.

Burt acknowledged that he was no lover of mankind. Maybe living in Europe would be...what?...less...hurtful. Aw, bullshit. Two years of Brooklyn College, getting into engineering, than saying screw it. The classes were interfering with his own education, taking up his time from reading what he wanted to read (how-to books, science mags and tomes about how the universe big-banged and is going to disappear into a black hole). Menial jobs here and there, in the back of stores fixing stuff; he knew how to fix clocks and watches and radios and typewriters and TVs. Right now he was out of work, but he was sure to hit it big with one of his inventions, especially on the latest plans he was drawing up for the miniature typewriter you could carry around in your pocket

His case against General Motors, the assholes of the auto industry, was another story. He knew he had them by the balls, if only he could find an honest judge. Anyway, he didn't have to spend millions on lawyers because he knew more about the case, the law, than even the judges. He still had some savings, barely, to live on.

The bus pulled into Plaza Colón. Burt got off, glanced up at ol' Chris Columbus on his pedestal and walked on past the San Francisco Church. The guy the locals called *El Oso* (The Bear), sat on the church steps. Ugh, that leg! It was about as thick as a tree trunk with skin like bark. And his pant legs were cut away, of course, to give the passing tourists enough of a view to make them sick and dig into their wallets and fill up the old plastic coffee cups lined up beside him. Why don't they pick up the poor guy and put him someplace? Probably couldn't, if he didn't want to go. They would let him stay out there, sickening tourists. That's democracy. Individual freedom. Beautiful.

He turned on San Justo, loping down to the post office-federal courthouse. He stopped in the lobby to go over the motion once more. People were collecting mail from the post office boxes there and he leaned against the ledge of one of the tall, barred windows that looked out to the street.

It read even better than he thought. He loved the phrase, "The pilfering of the idea of an honest, lone citizen by a greedy capitalistic giant denigrates the initiative of the individual, and should be judged a crime against the capitalist system that professes to hold the rights of individuals on the highest pedestal."

Burt climbed the marble staircase to the clerks' office on the second floor, where he filed his motion for reconsideration. As usual, he got a forced smile from Georgina, the clerk. She always plastered that smirky grin on her droopy face when he came up to the counter. He knew what she was thinking: *Here's that jerk again, another in forma pauperis filing, not costing this beggar a cent.* Yeah, but she was never really nasty. Face it, she was always patient, even helping that first time to fill out the form that got the free filings.

Next stop, La Bombonera up on San Francisco Street, for a soft-boiled egg, toast and the best coffee in town, brewed by that huge metal coffee machine made in Cuba way before the revolution. It was a great steaming, perking, metal thing of many cylindrical, levered and piped parts.

He sat at a small table in the rear, eyeing the outsized, middle-aged tourists coming off the cruise ships; two were taking up booths for four, going to the cash register to pay their bills, powdered sugar from the mallorca sweet rolls around their blubbery mouths. At a table across from him, four local seniors in white and blue guayaberas were laughing and arguing—probably about politics. That's all they think about. Independence, statehood or stay as they are, called commonwealth. What the hell was the difference?

Politicians would still be running the place. Money would rule.

When he first came down here, there were nice things around the island, the mountains, like Switzerland in the Caribbean, fishing villages such as Boquerón, where they sold those sweet little oysters right along the street, the people out on the island, poor and friendly, sharing stuff. But whatever Puerto Rico becomes, the same old crooked jerks will be running things.

Well, at least there was Luz. Luz was the closest ever to someone he wanted to see again. *Show me the light, Luz, like you done before.*

Burt spent the afternoon at the Carnegie Library. Last night, he decided he would again dive into research to pick up the beneath-the-radar connections of other General Motors wrongdoings that he would use to bolster his case. But what he found was mostly what he already had on GM—newspaper and magazine articles about tax fraud, fighting unions coming to new plants in the South, the old one about hiring private dicks to spy on Nader's private life, and all the suits against the jackasses of Detroit for putting Chevy engines in its Oldsmobiles, instead of the supposedly great Olds "Rocket" engines. Too bad GM hadn't recently stolen anything from other inventors, like Ford, Chrysler, or do what the other assholes did to that guy who invented the intermittent windshield wiper. Maybe he'd contact the windshield wiper guy and they would team up for another lawsuit against the whole crooked auto industry. *Not a bad idea,* thought Burt, wiping his dripping nose.

After leaving the library, he walked around to work up an appetite. He went to the top of the Old City, then along the street there, passing the old walls and the fort that protected the island from the British and the Dutch invaders. But those walls or nothing else, were able to stop Tío Sam from taking over the island—lock, stock and every which way. So the PRs just fell for the Yanqui bullshit about progress, democracy and making money. Besides, they could always come up to the states and go on welfare.

Still, poor was poor, and Bert felt for all poor people, like the ones living below the wall in those cluttered-together shacks that sloped all the way down to the ocean. Poor fuckers. Except, maybe it was better being poor here than in New York. The rich, of course, were doing more than all right. Well, they always do, even here, where they live in their beachfront mansions and condominiums. The rich get richer because the poor get screwed, every which way. So, what, Burt Cherry, is your philosophy of life? Who the fuck knows? What he does know is that he has been screwed out of almost everything almost all of the time, which makes him cynical, to say the least.

He walked along Boulevard del Valle to the San Cristobal Fort, then, headed down the hill back to the Plaza Colón. Dusk was settling in. Then, like always in the tropics, night came on before you knew it. He wound up in the Chinese restaurant on San Justo and ordered wonton soup, chicken chow mien, an egg roll and tea. It was nothing to write home about—if he had a home to write to. A $6.50 meal, a $1 tip. He still had an hour or so before he would see Luz. He wanted her to get settled in before he went over there.

More walking, then down to the waterfront where the monster liners were docked for the bloated tourists, waiting for them to buy their made-in-Bangladesh T-shirts saying 'Puerto Rico' on the front. Lights were strung along the decks of the liners, whose horns hooted like electrified cow moos, getting ready to sail to the next tourist trap. Burt, in his mind, told the ships' captain to put the goddamn lights out so the passengers could get the full effect of the brilliant stars in the clear blue-black sky as they sailed out.

Nah, they'd probably be stuffing themselves inside with their sixth meal of the day. Burt Cherry on a cruise up around the Arctic Circle. See the Northern Lights streaming and swirling in the night sky. Maybe a rich widow aboard, looking for an intelligent companion, a guy who could explain about the collision of gas particles from the Earth's atmosphere with charged particles from the sun. First, jokes about himself and, gradually, she gets to like him.

He passed a large freighter and light-cargo boats that sailed between the islands. The moon stretched a long, gleaming path on the otherwise black lacquered bay. He finally came to "the place" and started up the stairs. Ridiculous murals were on the walls: a curvy, young babe dancing in a see-through sarong, accompanied by a guy in accordion-sleeves playing the conga drum; flamenco babes whirling and bursting out of their costumes; barefoot, grinning, maracas-shaking peasants, the guys in straw hats, the babes in Carmen Miranda headpieces. The place was packed with guys that came off the ships, tourists and locals. The steel band of five guys in gold shirts were clanking out sounds from a revolving stage above and behind the bar. If it wasn't for Luz he would never set foot in such a joint.

He and Luz had met in the Condado, in front of one of the tourist hotels, where he had dropped fifty hard-saved bucks in the casino, cursing himself for going there in the first place. Okay, he had to try it once, didn't he? Anyway, she was there and he was there and her smile went right through his stomach and into his...other parts. And that's when they met. Later, she told him the places where she worked on different nights. Tonight, Friday, was at the loft-sized place called, the Latin Quarters Nite Club.

He waited at the door looking for her, seeing the whores in their mini-skirts swishing their asses around the floor, patting knees and grabbing other parts of the guys who sat around the bar. The steel band's clinking and clanking finally stopped and Burt went up to the bar. He ordered a scotch on the rocks from the head-shaved, tattoo-armed, hoop earringed, crooked-nosed bartender. He shoved the hands of the whores off his knees and other parts.

Finally, *finally,* she arrived. Her ample-hipped, heavy-legged, olive-colored, dark eyed, wide-nostriled, thick-lipped, frizzy-haired, wonderfully swollen-titted self. She stood in the doorway, as he had done, casing the joint with a terrific scowl. He tried to catch her eye, but couldn't, and pulled himself off the bar stool. He went halfway across the floor. "Hey!" he called. "Hey!"

She didn't hear him. Or maybe she did and made believe she didn't. Anyway, she was looking and scowling over his head.

He revved it up. "Hey Luz! Luz, hey!"

This time she looked at him. Her eyes drilled through him, then she smiled. A hint of gold glinted in the back of her mouth. He liked the way she was dressed. She wore just a plain white dress reaching below her knees, buttons down the front and a black belt around the waist. On her ears were black dots. There was a simple black bracelet around one wrist, a small black purse under her arm, regular heels—very un-whore-like.

"You wanna drink?" Burt asked.

She nodded, then came up to him and patted his arm. She sat at a table while he went back to the bar, picked up his drink, waited for her DonQ rum on the rocks, and paid for both. He saw that he had just enough money left, then brought the drinks over to the table. Just a few how's it going's and *buena-buena's* were exchanged, then finishing off their drinks, and they were on their way.

Outside, she took his hand and led him to a hotel around the comer. They rode an elevator up two flights and went to a reception desk where he paid the $5 to the old, skinny, under-shirted, faded-tattoo-armed desk clerk, who told him *"quarto diez."* They went down to the end of the hallway and entered the room with the ten scrawled in paint on the door. Luz slid the door bolt inside and flicked a switch that started a ceiling fan going.

"You want the light?" she asked.

The room was partially lit by a streetlamp outside the window. "No *Luz,* just you, Luz," he said with half a smile. The fan rippled the gauzy white window curtain. She took a deep breath and put out her hand.

He dug into his wallet and took out the twenty. After taking it from his hand, she put it into her purse, then slipped out of her dress, folded it across the room's one chair, stepped out of her panties and undid her bra. He saw those over-plump, light brown breasts with the fully rounded, seemingly winking nipples and something inside his head started spinning. His mouth went dry and his fingers tingled.

"You get undressed?" Luz asked, giving him a look that he was sure said, "Come on, let's get this over with."

He pulled off his shirt, toed off his loafers, got out of his pants and jockeys, but kept on his socks. He thrust his mouth on one nipple, then the other. He buried his head between her breasts. He felt the juices flowing inside him.

Then he looked up and called Luz, *"Mi amor."*

Burt Cherry started singing the old Spanish song that was also a hit in English when he was a kid:

> Amor, amor, amor
> This word so sweet, that I repeat
> Means I have adored you.
> Amor, amor my love . . .

Luz looked down at him and smiled. "You my sweet man," she said.

What a bunch of balony!

But close enough.

Five minutes of love.

Everyone needs love.

Robert Friedman

Chapter 4

Margie was standing in front of her bar stool at the Solimar Guesthouse tapping her foot, trying to catch Perry's eye just to wink at the cute jerk. He wasn't looking her way—probably on purpose.

She had come to the island five years ago to try to kick her drug habit. She was still trying—and making progress, *gracias a Dios*. Margie waited tables at one of the tourist hotels and was on call for "escort services." She had no problem with that. Her earnings allowed her to rent a studio apartment in a beachfront condominium and drive a fire engine red Ford Mustang convertible. One problem she did have was her abiding crush on Perry, the bartender.

One night, after Perry had politely spurned her advances and had taken a break in the bathroom, Margie went behind the bar, picked up the baseball bat kept there "for emergencies" and smashed several bottles of whiskey, then left without a word. She returned two nights later with a guy wheeling in a dolly loaded with cartons of twice as many liquor bottles as she had broken. She abjectly apologized to Bernardo and Perry, presenting each of them with a bouquet of roses, saying she had been high on coke and rum-and-coke and didn't know what the hell she'd been doing. Bernardo was not amused, but Margie was grudgingly forgiven.

Having spotted Bernardo at a table on the patio, she picked up her little brown purse and the paperback she was currently reading in one hand, her Cuba Libre in the other, and approached him. "I gotta talk to you," she said.

Bernardo stood, went to the other side of the table and pulled out a chair for her.

"Why are you so polite?" she said giving him her sort-of-shy, lopsided grin, to see if she'd get a sincere response. When Bernardo openly smiled back, she turned on the beautiful, gleaming white smile.

Margie, dressed in white shorts and a blue halter and sandals, crossed her legs, inspected a blemish on her knee, then looked past Bernardo to Perry who was behind the bar. She knew her deep tan was attractive and she had just curled her shoulder-length black hair. She knew that her strong-boned features and smooth skin gave little or no hint of the rough going she had experienced in her life. Well, she was still in her twenties (twenty-eight and three months).

"What are you reading?" Bernardo asked.

Margie switched her glance to her book lying on the table and turned it so Bernardo could read the title: *One Arm and Other Stories* by Tennessee Williams. She was never without a paperback, whether it was a novel by Harold Robbins, Jacqueline Susan, García Marquez or Dostoyevsky. One evening, when Bernardo saw her toting *Crime and Punishment* to the bar, he pointed to the book and asked: "You believe in redemption through suffering?"

"Hey, don't spoil the ending."

"You like his plays?" Bernardo asked of Williams.

"I hated him for all the tortured women in them until I realized they were him, so now I can put up with them."

Then Margie's coffee-colored eyes locked onto Bernardo's. "What's with that Perry character?" The literary talk was over; she had more pressing matters to discuss.

"What do you mean?" Bernardo said.

"Well, how come he doesn't melt before me like all the other johns I come on to?"

She cocked her head toward the bar where Perry was nodding his shaven head, squinting his pale blue eyes and pruning his surprisingly heart-shaped lips. That crazy guy who usually only talked to himself at the bar was now recounting some real sad story to Perry, who had his sympathetic bartender's face on, waiting patiently to instantly forget whatever he was being told. As he half-listened, his muscular, tattooed arms washed out glasses and wiped down the bar.

Margie took a healthy gulp of her drink. "Hey, Perry's weird," she said. "I mean like I've had the head creeps of the biggest banks on the *Milla de Oro* and soap opera *guapos* fall in love with me after a night on the town and in their beds—all of them, by the way, little boys who want to be told what great lovers they are, even the ones that last thirty seconds. But, anyway, why can't I get to first base with freckle-face behind the bar?"

"Perry may be a much different type of man than you're used to."

"He's gay, isn't he?"

"Not necessarily."

"Oh, not *necessarily?* What's that supposed to mean?"

"At this point in his life," Bernardo said, "I think Perry isn't too sure about…lots of things."

"So, let him join the club." Margie finished off her drink and went to the bar for another.

"How's it going?" she asked Perry.

"It's going," Perry said.

"Hey, you want to go out sometime?"

"Sure."

"Great! When?"

"Sometime."

"You're something else…like weird." Margie's smile was

really a frown. She picked up her drink and returned to the table to Bernardo. She took a deep gulp of her rum-and-coke. "Give me a half hour alone with him and..."

Bernardo shook his head.

"What's the matter, don't you believe in love?"

Bernardo sipped his cognac. He said nothing.

"Well?" Margie's jaw started working.

When Bernardo didn't answer again, Margie said: "Love, sex, gay, straight. One doesn't have to do with the other, or it's all mixed together, right? I mean, the most important thing is that, when it's for real, when two souls are reaching out... what the hell. It could be kisses or hugs or just holding each other, or doing everything else, you know? You see what I'm trying to say, about the gay thing, about l-o-v-e?"

Bernardo nodded. "I understand," he said. "I really do." There was a pause, then Bernardo said, "I really should call it a night."

Margie reached over and took one of Bernardo's hands in her own. She kissed his hand, then let go. "It's time for me to disappear, too."

She stood and went back to the bar, called out loudly to Perry, who was in the little kitchen fixing a sandwich for a customer and he poked his head out. She gave him a soft, *"Buenas noches, mi amor"* and he gave her a little wave.

Such a little fruity wave of the fingers for such a big guy.

Margie went back across the patio and out the front door.

Two nights later, Margie arrived at the guesthouse bar with Eddie Feliciano in tow. Feliciano was a local financial whiz kid and a leading playboy-about-town, according to the local newspapers. He was about forty; short, dark and fairly handsome; a bachelor who, according to the *chisme* (gossip) around town, *juega a los dos bandos* (swung both ways sexually). Margie couldn't care less.

In her three-inch heels, she had several inches on Eddie as they strode up to the bar, then mamboed and cha-cha-ed to Tito Puente recordings played on the old-fashioned juke box. Margie, in her tight red mini-dress, shook, dipped and wiggled in a clearing she had directed Eddie and Perry to make by moving unoccupied tables around on the patio.

Margie was already flying high when she entered the guesthouse. She kept tripping off to the ladies' room, while her black-tie escort knocked down several scotch-on-the-rocks. She introduced Eddie to Perry as "my lover man who has contracted my services forever." She then proceeded to begin her overriding mission for the night: to tease and taunt the bartender.

"You had a chance, but you missed out," she told Perry.

"Too bad you weren't...um, up to it."

Perry answered: "Yup."

Toward midnight, when only she and her escort were on the other side of the bar, she invited Perry to dance to a Tito Rodriguez bolero, and when he declined on the grounds that he would be having a good time on someone else's dime, she replied: "Hey! I'm asking you to dance with me, not lay me."

"Maybe he just don't want to be *into* you," Eddie Feliciano said. He gave Perry a wink and a little pursing of the lips, to say: "You know what I mean, right?"

Perry checked his watch. "Time to close the bar," he said.

Then Eddie said to Margie, with an eye on Perry: "Hey, you know how we can all make up and come together? How about a three-way, *mi amor?* "

"Pervert!"

"You know you'd love it."

"Get lost."

She asked Perry: "Could you call a cab for me?"

"Hey, *bitch,* " said Eddie Feliciano, "who took you to dinner and a show at the Tropicoro Club in the El San Juan Hotel and gave you the shit you been sniffing in the ladies' room all night? Now you owe me. We came together, we're going back to my penthouse condo overlooking the world and you're gonna lick whipped cream off my dick."

"The only thing I'm gonna do with your dick," Margie said, "is twist it around so it can go up your ass, which would be the greatest favor any woman could ever do for you."

Eddie got off the bar stool, weaved back and forth, looked down at his fingers, then put them around Margie's neck and began to choke her.

Perry didn't bother coming through the short swinging door at the side of the bar; knees bent, he leapt onto the bar, as though it were a pummel horse, then dove off, the heel of his hand smacking against Eddie's flat forehead, sending him spinning. Eddie dropped his own hands behind him trying to break his fall. He struggled to his feet and ripped off his black bowtie and threw it to the ground, as though he was ridding himself of a major impediment to whatever would follow. Five foot, five-and-a-half-inch Eddie Feliciano moved up to muscular, six-foot Perry and said: "Okay, motherfucker, first I'll beat the shit out of you, then I'll fuck you."

Perry's pale blue eyes opened wide. He took the deepest of breaths, pulled his head back and peered at the stars. Then he looked back down and, with an index finger, wagged Feliciano away. "I'll get a taxi for you," he told Margie.

Feliciano picked up his bowtie and pocketed it. He stalked through the small lobby and out the front door.

Perry made calls at the front desk, then came back. "I

tried two taxi services. One was busy, the other didn't answer. We'll walk a little down Ashford," he said. "A cab is sure to come along."

Perry closed up the bar and they started down the avenue. A few blocks down, a black Jaguar convertible skirted around a corner and pulled up to them. The front passenger door shot open. "Get in!" Eddie Feliciano ordered Margie.

"Fuck you!" said Margie.

"Bitch, we got a contract. I agreed to pay your rent for the next month and to keep you in the shit you sniff. I gave you a goddamn check. Get into the goddamn car!"

"Fuck you," Margie repeated.

Eddie drove the Jaguar up onto the sidewalk. Perry led Margie around the back of the vehicle. Eddie revved the car back into the road and blocked their path again.

Margie jumped back. "You almost hit us, you moron!" She smacked a fist on the front fender.

"Touch my car again and I'll turn you into road kill!"

Perry took Margie's hand and led her back to the sidewalk and Feliciano drove slowly beside them, shouting: "Get in the car, *puta!*"

Two cars behind began honking their horns. Feliciano was screaming: *"¡Puta! ¡Puta!"*

Now Perry's face hardened. "Shut up," he told Eddie. "Move out!"

Feliciano braked and swerved halfway onto the sidewalk again. The cars behind bucked and weaved and continued to blare their horns as they squealed out down the road. Feliciano went to the glove compartment; out came a blue-black pistol.

"You're the one moving outta here," Feliciano told Perry, pointing the gun at his stomach. "Disa-fuckin-ppear or you are one dead, useless bartender."

Margie's mouth slowly opened wider and wider, then she let out a scream that soon blended with the whoop of a siren. She stopped screaming as the siren moaned, like a dying animal. Two cops came warily out of the patrol car, their pistols drawn.

"¡Suelta l'arma! ¡Sueltala!"

As ordered, Eddie dropped the gun onto the passenger seat. "All I'm trying to do is defend myself against these two, who were trying to rob me! I was giving them a ride and they threatened me and wanted my money."

"That's a bunch of bull!" Margie said.

Eddie said, "Can I give you my card?" He began to reach into his jacket, but one of the cops, pointing his gun, waved his hand away.

"Hey, I'm not gonna…"

"Keep your hands out!" the cop said.

"He's a goddamn liar!" Margie said.

The other cop went around to the front seat of Feliciano's car and picked up the handgun and pocketed it. Perry was frisked, then cuffed to Margie.

"What the hell is this?" Margie said. She and Perry were pushed into the back of the squad car. Feliciano was told to sit up front.

"What about my car?" he asked, before getting into the patrol car.

"Park it against the curb," one of the cops said.

Feliciano pulled the car off the sidewalk and put it in a no-parking zone. He got back in the patrol car between the two cops and they drove off.

As soon as they got to the police station, Feliciano announced that he wanted to make a phone call. He was allowed the call. The person on the other end of the line spoke to the arresting officer, who kept nodding and saying, *"Sí, señor. Sí, señor. "*

The upshot of the call was that the police decided that Feliciano, who said his license for his weapon was at his apartment, was indeed under threat. He was released and his weapon returned to him. One of the cops said he would be given a ride back to his car.

"What the hell?" Margie said again. "That jackass started it all!"

The cops ignored her.

After another half hour of sitting on a bench across from the desk sergeant, Perry and Margie were uncuffed and Margie was told she was free to go.

"Come on, Perry," she said.

"He stays," said the desk sergeant.

"What d'ya mean?"

"Those are my orders, lady."

"I ain't leaving unless…"

"Go," Perry said. "Get me a lawyer, or something."

Margie stalked out of the station. Incredibly, Feliciano was waiting for her, in his convertible. He opened the front door.

"C'mon, I told the police that you didn't do anything, it was your buddy who threatened me. I forgive you. Let bygones be gone. C'mon, we'll spend the rest of the night at my place. I got more *perico* there."

"Get lost, creep," Margie said.

Feliciano cocked his head back, as though he were actually surprised by Margie's reaction. He looked at his glove compartment, seeming to contemplate retrieving the gun. Instead, he squealed off in his car, screaming at the top of his lungs: *"¡P-u-t-a!"*

Margie walked all the way back to the guesthouse. She rang the bell, once, twice, again and again. A bleary-eyed Bernardo opened the door.

"Hey, I'm sorry," Margie began, "but Perry's got a problem. He's locked up in the police station for trying to help me." Bernardo took a long, deep breath.

"We got into a fight. Not with each other, with that sonovabitch Eddie Feliciano. Eddie pulled a gun on us. The cops took us all in. Then they let us go, except Perry. They're keeping him there. I don't know what for."

"What happened?"

"Hey, I just *told y*ou!"

"Where is Perry now?"

"At the station house on Loiza Street. He didn't do anything, except try to help me. Someone's got to talk to the cops and find out what's going to happen to him."

Margie read Bernardo's mind. He was going to say, "Not now, tomorrow."

"It has to be now. I don't think Perry speaks Spanish too good so he may get himself into more trouble."

They took Bernardo's car, which was parked in front of the guest house. When they got to the station, Bernardo told the desk sergeant he was Perry's employer and asked if he could be informed about his employee's status, since he would need to find someone else if Perry couldn't show up for work early the next day. The sergeant looked suspiciously at Margie, then referred Bernardo to the arresting officer, who told Bernardo that Perry was being held for a court hearing in the morning on a charge of attempted assault.

"Hey, that's bull!' said Margie. "He didn't assault nobody. *We* were the ones who the gun was pulled on.*"*

"Please lady, don't curse," the officer told Margie.

"You saw it," Margie told the arresting officer. *"You* made Feliciano drop his gun."

The cop shrugged. "I'm only following orders," he said.

"Look," said Bernardo, "there must be some sort of misunderstanding here."

"That's for the judge to decide," the police officer said. "We'll be taking the suspect to the Hato Rey Judicial Center for an arraignment at seven a.m."

"Where is he now?" Bernardo asked.

"In a cell in the back."

"Can we see him?"

"Negative," said the desk sergeant. "Not allowed, unless you're his lawyer."

Bernardo drove Margie to her condo. They were to meet at seven in front of the courthouse.

After about three hours of sleep, Margie pulled up to the judicial center in a taxi. Bernardo was waiting by the stairs leading into the courthouse. Margie wore a yellow blouse, jeans, heels, and sunglasses that took up half her face. She shouldered a large black leather bag.

Perry pled not guilty to simple assault—no mention was

made of a weapon—and the judge set bail at $5,000. Bernardo signed over a $500 check he had received for rent from Don Cisco, one of his boarders, to a bail bondsman and Perry was released, pending a later hearing.

"Take the bail money out of my salary," Perry told Bernardo.

"It's a loan. When you have it, you can pay me back. No hurry."

Perry nodded and thanked Bernardo. He then thanked Margie for showing up for the court hearing.

"Hey, I feel guilty as hell," Margie said. "It's because of me that you got into this mess. *I* should be asking how I could pay *you* back." Margie searched Perry's face, as though seeing something there that would show her a way.

"No problem," said Perry.

Bernardo bought them breakfast in the courthouse cafeteria, then said he had to pick up some new door locks at the hardware store in Santurce. Would they mind going there before they took them home? Margie said *no problema*, she and Perry would catch a cab. Margie kept rubbing Perry's knee on the ride back. Bernardo exited first and Margie told the cabbie to take them to her condominium. Perry said nothing.

They moved back down Ashford and pulled up a block from the Condado Beach Hotel. Perry dug into his pocket, but Margie, who already had a twenty out, slapped his hand in his pocket and paid the cabbie.

The tiled floor in the small lobby had been sleekly polished. They got into the elevator and it shot smoothly up to the fifteenth floor. When they arrived at the door to her place, Margie dug into her black bag, took out a small ring of keys and snapped open the bottom, then the top lock. She held the door open for Perry and they entered.

"Hey, I didn't make the bed this morning!" she said, as though surprising herself.

Perry looked down at the large fold-out couch that took up about one-third of the room and grunted. Then he grinned.

"I didn't do the dishes either." Margie frowned at the sink in the small kitchenette across from the bed. "And look at these damn clothes all over the chairs and everything."

"Like I care," said Perry.

"Okay, but look at this," she said, taking Perry by the hand and leading him to the sliding window doors beyond the sofa-bed. She opened the doors. "Come on. Look."

The view from the small balcony was all beige beach, sky-blue sky and blue-green sudsy sea.

"You wanna a drink out here?" she asked, tentatively, as though thinking a drink along with the view might be too much for Perry.

"Sure."

"What would you like? Scotch, vodka, rum, a daiquiri,

maybe a beer?

"A beer would be fine."

"That's what I want, too. Already, it's hot as hell, it's not even noon." Margie scratched away the sweat mustache forming over her lip.

They sat drinking their beers, looking out to the far edge of the ocean, where a freighter sat like a cutout waiting to be slid along a stage. Perry closed his eyes.

"You're tired, right?"

Perry nodded. "Bumpy, cruddy mattress and they leave the lights on all night in the cells."

"You wanna lie down?"

"I would appreciate that."

"Okay, let me fix the bed."

Perry followed Margie inside and helped her smooth out the sheets. It was cooler inside with the air-conditioning. Perry sat on the edge of the bed, kicked off his loafers, smiled sheepishly and plopped down, his legs splayed, his bare feet pointing to the ceiling. "Whew! *Muchas gracias.* Just a quick nap."

Margie put her hand on the big toe of Perry's left foot. She rubbed it softly and looked into Perry's eyes, smiling. Perry blinked rapidly. He closed his eyes. Margie let go. Perry turned on his stomach.

While Perry slept, Margie called the restaurant where she had the 4 p. m. to midnight shift and told the manager she was taking the day off. She had a bad cold and didn't want to sneeze over the customers' food.

"Take care, drink hot rum with lemon," said Jaime, the manager. He was a good guy.

She put away the clothes scattered around the room. Her goddamn closet was packed. It was time to give away some dresses and shoes to the other waitresses. Suzie was her size. Suzie was a sweet kid finishing up at the University, studying to be a social worker, which was what Margie had wanted to study until…

She was cutting down, would soon be off it. Just the coca now. Just a little. She'd be clean…soon.

As quietly as she could, she washed the dishes, scrubbed the bathroom floor and sink, swept, dusted and mopped, and kept looking at Perry, to make sure he wasn't being woken. He was out like a light. She showered and changed into cut-off jeans and a loose, sleeveless white top.

Where did she put it? She went to the first drawer under the sink. The knives, forks, spoons—Woolworth, expensive plastic—all spoons bunched together. She had to put them in separate compartments. What the hell was wrong with her for so long? She pulled out the next drawer. All kinds of crap—bottle openers, keys, corkscrews, pliers, corks, scissors, nails, a hammer, pens, buttons, toothpicks, matches, loose cigarettes. Last drawer: some printed stuff, take-out menus, and deals on pizza deliveries. She crumpled them up and threw them in the trash can. She went back to the drawer, back in the back—there it was! Abuela Ceci's scrawls: *"jamón serrano, cerdo, sal,* olives, tomato, green pepper, sweet chili pepper, onion, *alcaparras,* oregano, *achiote,* tomato sauce, garlic. Cook two hours, no less."

Gracias, Abuela Ceci. Thank God for the weekends at her house on Webster Avenue. *Mami* didn't cook for shit. She was too busy being dressmaker to the rich bitches downtown. Abuela Ceci cooked up a storm and had always listened to Margie's never-ending bitching. She was always in sympathy, putting frail arms around her, always there for her, kissing, laughing, crying. Margie had loved her grandma like mad and still loved her—in her grave. She hoped she still remembered how A*buela* taught her to do what turned out to be Margie's one expert dish. She had to start cooking again!

She went to her shoulder bag, dug out her wallet, and pulled out a bunch of twenties. She took out a pen from the bag and looked around for some paper. She picked up the top paperback from a pile on the table near her sofa-bed, tore off half a blank page at the back of the book and wrote on it: *Don't go nowhere. I'll be right back.*

She put the note on the bed near the formerly stroked

toe. Perry was whistling softly in his sleep. Margie closed the front door quietly without locking it then, walked the several blocks to the Pueblo Supermarket, where she got what she needed: a whole chicken, most of the other ingredients, some coconut flan (unfortunately she didn't have Abuela Ceci's recipe for that). At least she had some short-grained rice at home. And she bought a bottle of good Spanish wine.

Perry slept through the sizzling on the stove. He slept through the rich, tangy smells of the cooking. He slept through Ismael Miranda and Cheo Feliciano singing low volume on the portable radio Margie brought over from the table by the bed.

She switched off the radio and took Orwell's *1984* and a beer out to the balcony. She sat in one of the two orange-canvas director's chairs out there. It was hot as hell, even though the balcony was now in the shade, and she rolled the beer bottle across her forehead and kept reading and reading. *Wow!* How many Big Brother-wannabees did she know in her life? Too friggin' many. She went back inside, checked on the chicken simmering on the stove, opened the wine. She poured out a glassful, took a loose cigarette from the drawer, lit it on a burner, went back out to the balcony.

She drank the wine. She smoked the cigarette. She watched the sea.

Okay, it's ready. Time to shine.

She reentered. Perry was on his back again. She tickled his toes. He smiled and turned on his stomach. She kissed him softly on his neck. Perry turned; his eyes shot open; he looked…surprised, even a little shocked. But then his eyes lit up and he reached an arm out for Margie.

Margie pulled away. "Hey, buddy. It's time to eat."

"Wow!"

"Yeah, wow. Come on, I made some great *arroz con pollo.* You're gonna love it. You *better* love it."

Perry blinked. He pulled himself off the bed. "The bathroom?"

Margie pointed to the door between the balcony windows and the clothes closet.

"I'll be ready in a jiffy," Perry said.

Moments later he was at the table. He dug in.

Never had he tasted anything so delicious, Perry kept telling Margie. He really, truly meant it. The wine was great. They finished the bottle. Margie made espresso on a small machine on the kitchen counter. While the expresso bubbled, they had some flan. When he praised the flan, she said with a wink: "Just a little something I also cooked up while you were sawing logs."

"Was I snoring?"

"Just a little."

They exchanged smiles. Perry's lips quivered a bit, then.

his eyes widened. "Hey, what time is it? I never got my watch back from the police station."

"It's about five. Why?"

"Oh, Jesus. I have to get home and shower and get to work. I can't let Bernardo down, especially after what he did for me this morning, putting up the money for my bail."

"One night. Big deal," Margie said. "You should take it easy after last night. If you want, I'll call him and…"

"No, I'll go to work."

Margie's mouth got smaller and she was about to say something, but Perry added quickly: "I'll come back here. It'll be after midnight, but I'll come back—if you want. I'll come back here."

Margie took a deep breath. She went to the counter and poured herself a little cup of espresso. Whatever."

"I…"

"Yeah?"

"I'll come back," Perry said. "To be with you."

"*Mi casa,*"Margie said. "*Es su casa.*"

At 12:15 a. m., Perry was back at Margie's apartment. At 12:20, they exchanged their first kisses, soul-to-soul. About ten minutes later, Perry said. "Before we go any further, I might as well tell you."

"Tell me what?"

"The only one who knows down here is Bernardo. I

told him about it last New Year's morning, after a party at the guesthouse. We were on the beach, sharing a bottle of cognac watching the sky turn pink and the sea look like satin."

"And?"

"Yeah, well..."

"Come on, what?"

"I got a dishonorable discharge from the Marines."

"So?"

"I was on a pass in Beirut. I was drunk and wound up in bed with this young street guy and the MPs caught us and I was transferred just one week before the Arab terrorists blew up my barracks. So, since then, I've no longer wanted to have sex with men, women o r teenage child, all of which I had a lot of sex with before." Then, with a gentle wonder in his usually gruff-sounding voice, Perry said: "I owe my life to this kid, with eyes as gentle as pure innocence." A tear streamed down just one of Perry's eyes.

Margie cradled his head. "Don't worry," she said. They started kissing again.

"I think I'm getting hard, Jesus!" said Perry.

Soon they were naked and under the sheets. Margie's tongue made sure Perry was upright, then put Perry inside her and eased herself on him as he lay on his back.

"Oh, Je-*sus!*

"Okay, Okay. Stay with me. Think of monkeys eating apples."

"*Je-sus, Je-sus, Je-sus!*"

Abuela Ceci, thought Margie. *You're my savior.*

Chapter 5

WASHINGTON, June 3—The director of the World Health Organization's AIDS program declared today that the global epidemic of the disease has entered a third stage in which prejudice about race, religion, social class and nationality was spreading as fast as the virus.

Fred Anderson slapped at the green bottle fly buzzing around the powdered sugar on his toasted and buttered *mallorca*. The palm of his hand tickled at the memory of catching them as a kid. He would catch him as a kid and pull off their wings.

"We are witnessing a rising wave of stigmatization: against Westerners in Asia, against Africans in Europe, of homosexuals, of prostitutes, of hemophiliacs, of recipients of blood transfusions," the official, Dr. Johnthan Mann, told the Third International Conference on AIDS. Further spread of the virus throughout the world is inevitable, Mann said, and fears of acquired immune deficiency has become "a direct threat to free travel between countries and, to the...

Continued on Page 24

Fred bit into the pastry and the melted butter dripped onto his chin. He wiped it away with a finger, licked the finger and took a good sip of his *café con leche.* The early morning sun shone through the thick-leaved mango tree that canopied half the patio of the Solimar Guesthouse and speckled the chipped and cracked red tiles. The smell of the sea, cool and fresh, not yet hot and salty, wafted in the air.

He didn't have to go to page 24. Itwasthe homosexuals and junkies who'd better find out everything about the disease, what they should do to take care. *Their problem. They'd better take care.*

He came down to Puerto Rico to get away from all the crap going on in New York, the capital of bad news, new diseases, muggings, killings, corruption, filth, panic. He heard that AIDS was pretty damn serious in Puerto Rico also, but there didn't seem to be the hysteria here like up in New York, where the queers influenced so many major industries—

fashion, theater, media, even parts of Wall Street, which he wouldn't have believed until he himself got there. He had no prejudice against them. Paul Barton, his immediate boss at MANDO, who was well-closeted until one night of after-work drinks at Harry's, was a stand-up guy, defending Fred all the way after the screw up on the leverage rate of the pound. The mistake was nobody's fault because nobody could get the precise information at the time of the trade. Even though foreign currency trading was taking off and twenty-year-old brokers were becoming millionaires, he quit. Which greatly pissed Kathy—and of course, Artie—off. Artie had been the one who had gotten him the job in the first place.

"Yeah, you were a pre-med dropout hippie until you married my sister and you had the twins. And you realized you needed the bread, which you always wanted, anyway. I could sense it. You were ready to drop out of dropping out. So you traded your 'freedom from The Man' for the free market, which is what real freedom is all about and which you couldn't handle."

Well, screw you, Artie, I just dropped out again. I'm sorry Kathy, but we both knew it was over a long time ago. I love the twins but, Jesus, you became one never-ending pain in the ass. Why wasn't I home right after work? Why wasn't I doing this or that? What was I thinking, why was I doing what I was doing?

Fred left Kathy with most of what he had. The boys would be all right; private schools, all the way. He'd visit them from time to time, bring them down to Puerto Rico for vacations.

He sure wanted a break from the nasty mess his life had become in these last years. But he couldn't cut himself off *completely*. To cut himself off completely would be…well, it wouldn't be Fred Anderson, who always wanted to know why he was for, though usually against, all that was happening. He had to know even if, he had to admit, he got the nagging feeling sometimes that his opposition came from his lifestyle at the time, rather than his deepest down conviction. He voted for a Reagan-second term, for Christsake! At the time he was a Reaganomics, trickle down, supply-side believer! So keeping his subscription to *The Times* made him feel… what…still in touch? But in touch with what? He wanted to drop out again, didn't he? The last three months since coming down here, he hadn't done diddly. Well, he was thinking about the Triple J bio.

Fred Anderson, who tried to convince himself that he wanted what his mom and dad wanted—to become a surgeon like his old man—then found his true calling as a hippie who made it not only to Woodstock, but also to Atlantic City a couple of weeks earlier. The AC Pop Festival was where he fell in love with Janis. He followed her to festivals, clubs.

He still planned to do the Triple J bio that would combine the lives of Janis, Jimmy Hendrix and Jim Morrison (all friggin' dead before thirty).

Kathy and marriage and money in the late seventies and panic and well, not hate, but something hollow, which really was worse, something sucking at his insides and he knew if he didn't get the hell out, he would collapse in on himself.

So, now, in the year 1987, it was all falling apart for the gays. Not his problem.

Hospital Panel to Order Policy on Ending Care
Washington, June 3 - The main agency that accredits hospitals in the United States said today that it would require them to have formal policies specifying when doctors and nurses may refrain from trying to resuscitate patients who are terminally ill. The new rules will force providers of health care to address the medical, ethical and legal issues of withholding care from patients who are irreversibly ill and likely to die within a few days…

Fred finished off his *mallorca* and drained the coffee cup. He wiped his mouth with the blue bandana he started using again as a handkerchief and kept reading.

…the delicate and emotional issue of when to stop trying to save terminally ill patients and let nature take its course.

Yeah, let nature do its thing, Fred thought after reading the article. *Cancer, heart attack, AIDS, whatever. You're born, you live, you die, and you try to keep the hassles and the heartaches to a minimum.*

The next morning, *The Times* was not delivered. Fred was deeply disappointed. Although he knew he would get two editions the following morning, it was as though a day had been wrenched out of his life. He was pissed. He still felt he had to keep up with the way the world, outside of himself, was unfolding.

The weather hadn't held up the delivery, something that only happened during winter snowstorms in New York or tropical rainstorms here in Puerto Rico. It was now spring and hot and sunny. The paper could still be delivered late in the day. Flights were sometimes late. The delivery boy might have called in sick. Delivery was promised at seven and it was half past. He went to the public telephone in the lobby and called the local delivery service. The line was busy. He tried again. Still busy. He looked at the reproduction of Picasso's "Guernica" on the wall near the telephone.

Dialed. Busy.

Carmencita was mopping down the lobby, singing *Baby Love*. He tried the number to the local delivery service again. Still busy. He stared angrily at the telephone, as though expecting an apologetic shrug, then slammed the receiver down.

"Buen día, Señor Ahndersoon."

Fred was greeted by Don Cisco, coming down the stairs for his morning walk. As usual, the old guy wore a white guayabera over sharply pressed dark slacks and a panama hat. His yellow-tinted eyes and his perfectly aligned false teeth gleamed as he greeted Fred with a grin that crinkled his ebony-colored face. He looked at least ten years younger than the eighty-three years he proudly told everyone he had made it to, so far.

"Did you read that wonderful article about Mr. Bellow?" Don Cisco asked, referring to an interview with author, Saul Bellow, in yesterday's *Times*. The newspaper was left every day at the front desk by guesthouse owner Bernardo, also a subscriber, for whoever wanted to read it. Don Cisco, a retired biology teacher, devoured newspapers, magazines and books. Fred had just skimmed the article, even though the author had spoken of freedom, love and art, stuff that once grabbed him.

"Mr. Bellow is always an eloquent spokesman on the

ironic aspects of human nature," said Don Cisco with an easy smile, as though he were commenting on the pleasantness of the day.

Fred nodded. Fingers in his stomach jabbed for his morning coffee.

Don Cisco rolled his eyes up into his head, then pulled them back down, as though he had recovered a searched-for mental scroll. "The writer, you remember, talks about Mr. Bellow's latest book, recalling that a botanist in the novel says the problem of radiation levels, dioxin and harmful waste are all very serious, but that he believes more people die of heartbreak than of radiation. And Mr. Bellow says that although the botanist is ridiculed for the statement, he believes that it is true!"

Don Cisco nodded slowly and continued to smile, seeming to savor the idea, not so much for its scientific accuracy thought Fred, but for its own soulful sake. "Well, that is a notion to be contemplated this morning."

Don Cisco tipped his hat and headed for the front door.

Fred went out to the patio. Carmencita was mopping down the cracked brick-red tiles, now singing in weird coincidence: *Nothing But Heartaches*. He went to the kitchen behind the bar and prepared himself a coffee, as early rising guests were allowed to do,

Sitting out there, under the mango tree, he thought

about Millie.

She was standing still, except her head was twisting around, looking at the signs—Uptown to the Bronx; Downtown and Brooklyn; F train to Queens; A train to Manhattan, etc. That first glance, the beauty of her, that lovely behind, those long shapely legs in that yellow mini skirt, the black shoulder-length hair fanning out over her lovely olive-skin shoulders and sleeveless white blouse. A thin, sensual face. Big, beautiful, confused brown eyes. Could he help her? She looked frightened.

"Where do you want to go?" he asked her.

"Loweastsaida, Foursite Street. Please, how I can get there?"

It took a while, but he figured it out: Lower East Side. Forsyth Street. That's where she was staying with her sister. "Come on, I'm going that way."

She had arrived from Puerto Rico two weeks ago. She was coming from an interview for a job as a waitress at a Latino restaurant, a job she had to take while she waited to find out if she was accepted as a graduate student at City College. She had a degree from the University of Puerto Rico in social work. She wanted to help Puerto Ricans in New York and others, to survive and to make good lives for themselves and their families. She always wanted to live in New York since a visit when she was ten years old and saw the city from the top of the Empire State Building. He sensed her sincerity and sweetness. She was not like those hippie "lovers of mankind" types he had known, some, professing all that love while being real assholes to those closest to them.

He got off the train with her and walked her to her sister's apartment house. She agreed to see him on her first day off from work. All that summer, she had never had a steady schedule, but they phoned each other and made last-minute arrangements. He took her to movies and they walked around the Village and ate at restaurants there. They went to the Village East (formerly the Fillmore East) for rock concerts and while he thought he would have a problem getting that sweet body into bed early on, the third date or so, she came to his Avenue C apartment, the muscles in her legs tightening as they walked up the five flights. She was as eager as he to make love on his funky single bed. The little money he got from the music reviews he wrote for *Rock Scene* and *The Voice* he spent on her, in cool Village restaurants, for baubles, bangles, etc.

Then, out of the blue, she had to return to Puerto Rico. Her mother was very sick, her two older brothers had their own families, she had to take care of *Mami*. She got the news about her mother the day after she learned she had been accepted for the master's program at City College.

Fred tried to hide his heartbreak. "Let's keep in touch," he said. He would write, phone, come down to the island to visit her. He took her to the airport. She was in tears. He kissed her tears while he cried inside.

Come, come on, come on,
Come on and take it. Take it!
Take another little piece
Of my heart now, baby!
Oh, oh, break it!
Break another little piece
Of my heart now, darling,
Yeah, yeah, yeah.
Oh, oh, have another little piece
Of my heart now...

Janis knew.

She wrote him, he never answered. She called. He told her he was coming down to visit, he never did. He loved her, but maybe he didn't. Then he met Kathy and it was time to get married, raise a family, get a job with a future. His parents were bugging him from Colorado to settle down.

The truth was, he really didn't know how to express to Millie how he felt about her. He had always been the one to break up with girlfriends since high school and then in college. Mostly, he would see what they had to offer, sexually anyway, then, after it got to be the same old same old, he broke it off. Then, in his hippie years, the faked coolness escalated, no long-term connections, you knew and she knew, you made it with each other because that was what was done. Even the girls were into that. No recriminations, soul met soul on equal terms, one soul was as good as the next because you were looking to hook up with the 'Great World Soul' everyone was a piece of. You just had to dig deep enough to find it. You were fucking *it*, the other body was the means to *it*.

Until Millie.

Milagros.

Miracle.

That was 1975—twelve years ago! He had been in his early thirties then and Millie was twenty-one. *She's probably married now with twelve kids*, Fred thought. *With a drooping ass and tits, putting up with a cheating husband.* Still, maybe he should try to find her, even after all these years. Maybe he doesn't know what he's talking to himself about and she's as sweet and soulful as ever and could mend a still-broken heart— maybe, maybe not.

He spent the rest of the day going and coming from the beach and the guesthouse bar for beers, waiting in vain for a late delivery of *The Times*.

The next morning, two editions of *The Times* were delivered to him. Fred felt a sense of relief—until he started reading the front page of the day-before edition.

Newly Detected AIDS Virus Detected Spreads
WASHINGTON, June 4—A second AIDS virus, previously reported spreading in West Africa, has been detected in Europe and Brazil, Dr. Luc Montagnier of the Pasteur Institute said in Paris today. The HIV-2 virus has now been detected in about 100 people in France, West Germany and Britain...

Enough of this acquired immunity crapo! He tossed the paper aside and picked up the day's edition.

Specter of Chernobyl Affecting Life in Bangladesh
DHAKA, Bangladesh, June 4—It is said here, adapting an old folk expression, that Chernobyl is seven seas and 13 rivers away from Bangladesh. But these days it seems much closer.

A nationwide panic over radioactive imported milk powder began when the Government announced that a 1,600-ton shipment of powdered milk from Poland, which was affected by the Chernobyl nuclear accident in the Ukraine in April, 1986, showed unacceptable high-levels of radioactivity. Officials said the shipment registered radiation levels higher than tile 300 Bacquerels...

Fred blinked several times to get the sun out of his eyes until he realized that he was in the shade of the table umbrella. Slowly and carefully, he folded the newspaper in half, then in quarters. He stood, left the patio and laid the paper on the front desk, then returned to his second-floor room. He went to the small refrigerator and poured a full glass of water. He downed it in one continuous gulp.

He picked up two t-shirts he had left draped over a chair and threw them into the laundry basket, then crumbled onto the bed.

His organs are glowing!

Did he just drink a glass of water or milk?

He panics and takes a taxi to Presbyterian Hospital. The emergency room is packed with others who have drunk the milk. He sees the path of the milk in the others. It lights up their alimentary canals—mouths, lips, tongues, teeth are luminescent through the esophagus, sections of the stomach and intestines, right into the anus. A keening women sitting next to him has applied a thick coat of lipstick to try to cover the neon-green around her mouth, but the combination of colors only produces a bruised purple-brown blackness.

Fred sees that he has a special problem. His digestive system isn't aglow. But a steady phosphorescence radiates, through the clothes from two other body parts: his heavily beating heart and his erect penis.

They wheel him into a room in the back. Doctors shake their heads as they see Fred's glowing state. He feels the agitated lub-dub of his heart, while his nervous system, on full alert, causes a continual dilation of the arteries, shooting blood into the tissues of his penis.

A nurse holds up a mirror for him. He sees his iridescent, pear-shaped heart vigorously pumping through his black t-shirt, and his swollen lime-green penis quivering and straining through his khakis. Yeah, he has a world-class boner. The doctors are concerned about his accelerating heartbeat. Fred is mortified by the throbbing day-glo bulge in his pants. His penis, it seems, is almost humanly begging for fulfillment, or to be put out of its misery.

They wheel him into a dark room, where he is x-rayed, then connected up to wires and slid through a beeping machine. Blood is drawn. He is told to pee into a bottle.

The doctors tell Fred that the constant pressure on his heart has made it weaken dangerously, that his heart is starting to become over-burdened by the non-stop, artery clogging, excitation of his gonads. Open-heart surgery would be useless because the root cause would remain. There was no way to eliminate the radioactivity that was drawn, like magnetized metal, to Fred's sexual glands. The doctors come to the extremely reluctant and painfully sad conclusion that radical surgery is required. In order to save Fred's heart from giving out, his penis will have to be amputated.

Fred lies on the operating table, scrubbed, shaved and sedated. The crawling, spider-like anxiety has been numbed, its tentacles withdrawn as it is forcibly shriveled in a corner of his brain. But he knows enough about how the mind works on the body that the tense fear will again stretch out and creep forward and reach its hairy tentacles through his medulla oblongata and down his spine and into each part of his body.

His penis, in a cutaway garment, stands at quivering attention, like a good, yet nervous, soldier. A nurse with a pale-green surgical mask below her beautiful large dark eyes that are rimmed by long curled eyelashes grasps the head of his penis with a soft, gentle, loving hand and a sweet tingle cuts through the numbness. A surgeon moves in with a slender instrument that gleams beneath the overhead light that is as brilliant and as blinding as a magnified sun.

Fred didn't know if he had fallen asleep. Of course he

had. He reached down. He was still there. What a goddamn dream! What was that all about? He knew what it was about. Deep down, he knew. It was about his whole messed up life.

Time to drop out of dropping out again, this time for real. It was time to start doing meaningful things, get a job, teach English, start on the Triple J biography. Start looking for Millie.

He'd search the housing projects in San Juan, the barrios out on the island, the gated communities, the hi-rise condos by the beach, the small towns up in the mountains, the fancy suburban homes, the shacks in the slums. Tomorrow, he'd start looking all over the damn island.

Millie told him of visits to her grandfather. The grandfather's name was one Fred would always remember: Bienvenido Rivera—Mr. Welcome Rivera! Bienvenido lived in the Old San Juan slum of La Perla. Millie had told Fred of her nervousness whenever she went there to visit him because of all the stories she'd heard about the place, the beatings, stabbings, murders, robberies, drugs. The inhabitants were poor and poorer, Millie had said, but she also mentioned their kindness and the strange, almost magnetic attraction the place had for her. A good place to start his search? Possibly.

Tomorrow.

Right after he read *The Times*.

Robert Friedman

Chapter 6

Pablo Cruz Phillips' lips move as he again relates to himself the horror behind his eyes. His body, he knows, is plunked on the stool at the guesthouse bar near the sea in Puerto Rico, but his head and his heart are still on the bare hills in Korea—thirty-five years later. How could that be?

Their arms, legs, ripped from their bodies, their faces blown away. He still sees all of it, almost every goddamn day! Climbing Outpost Kelly, trying to get back that goddamn hill, all rocks and no cover.

Slaughter.

Bobby Campos falls on a live grenade, saving his buddies, Pablo included. Being sent out again to more slaughter. The Americano officers actually cut off their rations of rice and beans. They're ordered to shave their mustaches. Then Jackson Heights happens. He's sent out again by the Americanos. That's it! Fuck 'em! Court martial. Then the pardon. Even MacArthur said he was proud of the

Borinqueneers.

His agony remains.

Pablo asked the fellow behind the bar for another double scotch. The bartender was a good guy who understood people, their passions, their hang-ups, their rages and desires and bitterness. He understood their needs. Sure, that was his job: to listen and to commiserate, to fake it, maybe. But Pablo felt deeply that Perry, the bartender, really was *simpático.*

That was more than he could say for the jackass at the other end of the bar, a Vietnam vet. And that's all he talked about, how he killed gooks and loved it. Asshole, moron, *pendejo, cabrón! He was a patriot, that's why he fought in Vietnam, to stop the commies. Jackass. He didn't understand a goddamn thing about history or colonialism. Why the hell were we fighting in U. S. wars? Because they own us.*

"Gimme another Heineken," said the *pendejo,* lighting a cigarette. "I wanna drink to all the faggots who are gonna die from AIDS." He looked over at Pablo and put a smile on his unshaven, jowly face. Pablo looked through the *pendejo,* who turned to the bartender.

"So what you think, Perry? Revenge from God? Getting back at them for takin' it up the ass?"

Perry cracked his knuckles and shook his head. "Damned if I know."

"Hey, hey," he called over to Pablo. "What do you think, *Papi?* Is God getting back at the *maricones?"*

Pablo looked down and mumbled. He didn't want to start an argument.

"Hey, he's talking to himself for a change," Paco told Perry. "He's still on the fuckin' Frozen Chosin." With two fingers holding his cigarette, he tapped the side of his head. "Hey, Dad, the Korean war is over. We won!"

Perry put up a hand, gave a little shake of the head. "He's okay. Let it be."

Pablo drained his glass, then asked Perry for another double.

"Closing time in five," Perry said as he picked up the glass, dumped the small cubes in the sink, washed out the glass, and used it to dig out more cubes. Then Perry poured a generous amount of Chivas Regal in the glass. Pablo drank half of it down.

"Come on, old man," said the fat jackass at the other end of the bar. "Let's hear what you keep telling yourself."

Pablo looked up and turned his head to the guy. "Zip up your mouth. You talk too much and everything that comes out of that hole is bullshit."

The guy pulled his head back. He scratched the unruly black curls on the top of his head and his eyes widened. "Wow! *El loco* actually remembers how to talk!"

Pablo finished off his drink, then got off the bar stool. Something inside his head, something weightless and freeing, was spiraling up and up. He moved toward the other end of the bar, grabbed a thick shoulder and squeezed.

"Hey, old man, you want a quick death?"

"Hey," said Perry. "Let's not..."

Pablo dug his fingers into the t-shirt-covered flesh. The guy pulled back. He took a drag, then killed his cigarette in an ashtray on the bar. "Hey, you old, crazy bastard!"

"You talk too goddamn much. You make my head ache. Just shut..."

"Pablo! Where have you been?" another voice cut in.

Pablo turned. As he did, he felt knuckles crashing onto his cheekbone.

Sarah screamed.

Pablo stumbled, fell to his knees, looked around dazed, then took a deep breath and got up. He wobbled around, turned to his antagonist and pulled back a fist. Perry rushed out from behind the bar, arms extended between the combatants. "Come on guys. We don't need this."

Sarah put herself in front of Pablo and hugged him. She turned her head and sliced dark brown daggers at his antagonist. "You should be ashamed!" she said.

"Hey, he started..."

"That's it!" Perry yelled at Paco. "The owner was nice

enough to let you back in here. You were *so* sorry,now, you're out again. I'm gonna talk to Bernardo. Don't bother ever coming back."

"Yeah?"

"Yeah." Perry said the word low, looking straight into Paco's glassy black eyes.

"I don't need this shithole." Paco got off his seat and left the bar.

"Sorry," Perry said.

"Yeah, no problem," said Pable.

"I haven't heard from you in weeks," Sarah told Pablo. "You got me really worried. Come on. Let's get out of here."

Sarah, a few inches over five feet, led six-foot-tall Pablo by the hand, across the patio, through the lobby and out the front door. When they got outside onto the small porch, Sarah took a hankie out of her shoulder bag and dabbed at Pablo's reddish, swelling cheekbone.

"Have you eaten lately?" she asked.

"I had something this morning, I think. Who the hell knows?"

"Will you come to my apartment for something? I'll make an omelet."

Pablo gave a little nod. Sarah took him by the hand again and led him to her car parked down the street.

"I've been in every bar in the Old City," she said after

they got in, pulled away and drove down Ashford Avenue. "Someone told me to try the guesthouses in Ocean Park. You given up on the Old City?"

"I don't live there no more," Pablo said. "I got a room in Santurce. It's half the price."

"Since when have you been concerned about saving money?"

"Since I've been broke."

Sarah raised her eyebrows as she gave Pablo a quick look, then turned her eyes back to the road. "Broke?"

"It's all gone. All I have now is what the government gives me. I still got the shrapnel in my back."

Pablo and his three sisters had inherited a huge fortune from their mother's family after Sylvia Phillips had put a noose around her neck when they were teens. The millions from Texas oil had poured down three generations.

Sylvia, who wrote poetry for a "living," had met Nestor Cruz while both were vacationing in Spain. She returned with him to Puerto Rico where they married, eventually. Nestor, a politician, started out as mayor of San Juan, eventually rising to Speaker of the House in the island legislature. Pampered Pablo was sent to private schools on the island and in the states, and was set to enter M.I.T. to study engineering. Then he did something stupid. Tired of having his life mapped out for him, he enlisted in the Army. It went all downhill from there.

His outfit, the 65th Infantry Regiment, which had been cited for bravery at the beginning in Korea, met with disgrace later. More than 100 of them, including Pablo, were arrested for refusing to obey orders.

You go up the hill with three platoons and only three guys come back. They send you up again with other platoons and again, three guys come back. They order you up that hill again. Fuck you, you go up there, they said, just like some of the "white" guys said, and nothing happened to them. But the no-spica-da-English PRs get court-martialed. Corporal Cruz Phillips gets two years hard labor. A couple of the sergeants get 18 years. Fuck the PRs.

Then clemency and pardons come from the Secretary of the Army in a way that it didn't look like the U. S. was doing what it was doing: screwing the PRs in war and in peace, and in just about every way that colonial and neo-colonial masters have screwed the natives down through the centuries.

After Army life, Pablo more or less did what he wanted, studying here and there, traveling, living in Paris and Madrid, drinking. His old man wanted him to follow the leader into politics. But Pablo didn't want to have anything to do with those jerks. Besides, he believed Puerto Rico should be independent and even though the old man felt the same, he wanted his son to run as a candidate in the middle-of-the-road party that the old man stuck with so he could get re-elected again and again. The old man ran for governor, lost, had a heart attack, died.

Pablo had some success painting war scene horrors. He saw a series of shrinks, and he drank and painted. He had less "success" as he moved on to abstracting the horrors in hot, ugly colors and shapes. No more suprarealist scenes. He opened a gallery, then closed it six months later. He didn't want to deal with other artists, who were incredibly stupid, stubborn and selfish (just like him). He drank, he painted portraits of his suffering self and of nonentities-about-town. By this time, he had pissed off the island art colony, which took some doing, and galleries refused to show, critics disdained and collectors didn't want to buy his works. More drinking, no longer painting.

He knew Sarah was the only good thing that had happened over those years, and Annie, their daughter. There were some years of happiness—full, quasi, then less and less —then misery set in. About five years ago, they decided they had to separate. Too many tears in the guts and through the ducts—too many threats, too much menacing silence. But never more than momentary hate on his part at least. It was best to live apart, see each other occasionally, weekly, possibly monthly.

They took the ocean road into the Old City. Two container ships sat low on the horizon like one-dimensional cutouts. How much more beautiful were the shapely, smoking freighters of Pablo's childhood. Sarah found a parking space on Calle San Justo, right in front of her townhouse off Boulevard del Valle. From her roof was a view of La Perla's slum dwellings, then, beyond, the sun-and-moon-glittering sea.

Blanche, the cat, meowed up a storm as they entered the house. Sarah rubbed her all over and Blanche purred. Pablo bent down to pet the cat and it scampered beneath the couch. *Screw you,* thought Pablo, then told himself not to be too judgmental, the cat hadn't seen him in a long time.

Pablo's paintings were still covering most of the walls of the two-story house (some of the abstracts, a few of the portraits). Other Puerto Rican paintings also hung there, and the posters of Sarah Figueroa as Blanche DuBois in *Un Tranvía llamado Deseo,* as Martha in *¿Quién le teme a Virginia Woolf?,* as Sally Bowles in *Cabaret* (Sarah had a terrific singing voice), and many others (Portia in *The Merchant of Venice,* Miranda in *The Tempest,* Bernarda in *La Casa de Bernarda Alba,* et cetera, et cetera).

Sarah set out plates, silverware, and napkins on the dining room table. "I'll make us Westerns now." She went into the kitchen.

Pablo wolfed down the omelet and *pan de agua* with

two cups of strong black coffee. He belched softly, then daintily tapped the napkin against his mouth.

"Feel better now?" Sarah asked.

"I feel much better," said Pablo, looking gratefully, even a bit shyly, at his wife.

"Like old times."

"Yeah," said Sarah. "You got to start taking better care of yourself. *Estás flaco*. You've got to eat regularly."

Pablo knew that Sarah knew not to mention his drinking anymore.

Then she told Pablo, "Annie is coming down to the island tomorrow with Betty, your granddaughter, and Carlos, your son-in law. Actually, that's why I went hunting for you tonight. I would like all of us to spend the weekend together."

Pablo mumbled something.

"What?"

"You want…uhm…that I stay here?"

"Let's be a family. It's just for a couple of days."

"They still running that gallery in Soho?"

"Yes," said Sarah. "The gallery has become quite popular. Mostly, they show works by exiles: Cubans, Russians, Haitians, Chileans, Vietnamese."

"No Puerto Ricans?"

"I suppose so, if Puerto Ricans in the states are considered exiles."

"What do you call them?"

Sarah didn't answer. She just smiled. "You will be around this weekend?"

Pablo smiled at his wife. "Sure."

"Do you want to sleep out here, on the couch, or with me in the bedroom?"

"What d'ya you think?"

"I don't know, that's why I ask."

Pablo's eyes became suspicious slits. Then they shot open and he pulled his head back and laughed. He took Sarah in his arms, tightened them around her. "I miss you so much, *mi amor.*"

"I bet," Sarah said.

Pablo kissed his wife hard on the lips, then more softly. Softer, and her mouth opened and their tongues touched. Like old times.

Sarah pulled back. "Okay," she said. "Let's get ready for bed."

Pablo went to the bathroom and peed. He leaned over the sink and threw some water on his face and rubbed toothpaste around his teeth.

They made love softly, sweetly, then fast and hard. Beautiful!

Then Pablo felt tears pressing; he held them in.

"You are my one love," he told Sarah.

Sarah sighed. "Still?"

"Always."

The next morning was not so beautiful. They sat at a small green table in the kitchen behind the dining room, dunking *pan de agua* into *café con leche.* Pablo was rubbing the five-day growth around his dimpled chin, saying nothing.

"You feeling all right?"

"I'm feeling like I feel," he finally said.

"Okay."

Then Sarah said, "I have to pick up Annie, Carlos and Betty at the airport in about an hour. Do you want to come with me?"

Pablo bit his lower lip. "What a bunch of bullshit!"

"What are you talking about?"

Pablo knew the expression of confusion that just washed over Sarah's face, was, of course, bullshit, too.

"You know what I'm talking about."

"What do you mean, *you* know. I *don't* know."

"Come on. All this family bullshit. After a while, it all comes closing in on you. You never win."

Sarah was tapping her foot. "Now you're losing me."

"Yeah," Pablo said. "We're all lost and I, for one, won't take this shit anymore."

Sarah blinked several times. "Oh, God!"

"Yeah, fuck Him, too."

Now he was *really* pissed off and hyperventilating. He stood and knocked over his mug of coffee. The coffee dribbled from the table down to the floor. He took his red bandana from the back pocket of his khakis and started mopping up the mess.

Even Blanche, the cat, who had been lapping milk from her saucer, went on the attack, sneaking over, arching her back and hissing at him before retreating under the couch.

"Leave it," said Sarah. "It doesn't matter. I'll mop it up."

"It matters," said Pablo. "Every *goddamn* thing matters. It all matters and I can't take it anymore!" He stomped on the bandana and rushed from the kitchen, through the living room and out the front door.

The one ceiling fan rotated drunkenly over the dozen or so barstools of the Mundomalo Saloon. In a corner by one of the six tables, a caged electric fan whined and rumbled, accompanying the jukebox version of Sammy Davis Jr. straining to know "What Kind of Fool Am I?" The air-conditioning was broken for a change and the fans spread dank odor and cigarette smells around the place along with a little air.

Pablo sat at one end of the bar. A noontime regular was bent over his poison in the middle. The tables were not occupied. Fritzie, the German floozy who worked the daytime shift, sat her squat body on a stool behind the bar, a cigarette hanging from her lips. She was concentrating, with a grimace, on filing her nails, like she was preparing a weapon.

Pablo jiggled the ice cubes in his Chivas.

Fritzie looked up.

"Another double, please," he said.

"Yah," said Fritzie. She held her hands out to admire her filing job, then poured Pablo his drink. "A little early for you, no?" she said as she brought him the drink. "I don't expect you till when the sun starts going." She leaned over and whispered, her butch-cut head jerking down the bar. "Not like dat one, he ain't left to change his underwear or nothin' in over the day and night."

Pablo looked at the guy whose head was down on his folded arms. He started snoring loudly.

Fritzie went up to him and tapped him on the head. "No snoring," she said with a smile. The guy pulled up his head. His middle-aged, deeply lined, almost respectable looking face was pallid and sweaty. He almost tumbled off the stool, then weaved over to the jukebox, studying the selections. He put in some coins and Sammy Davis Jr. returned with the same questioning song. The guy stumbled off to the bathroom.

Pablo finished off his third double, threw down several bills and left the bar.

He walked down Calle San José to the Plaza De Armas

and sat on a bench across from City Hall. His head was pounding. *That's what morning drinking does—makes your head pound, and loosens the bowels.*

Then came more discomfort. He could feel the heat rising to his face.

One day after school, so many years years ago, he was running around the Old City with Gabby and Pedrito. They came to the plaza. He saw his old man walking along the second floor arched balcony of City Hall.

He called up to him. *"¡Papi! ¡Papi!"* His old man stopped, looked over the railing, spotted Pablito, waved to him, then shouted, "Go home and do your homework," then walked on. Everyone was laughing. Pablo tried to smile, felt himself blushing, and ran home.

Weird. It meant nothing. Meant everything. Now it weakened him again. The memory drained everything from his body, while filling his head with embarrassment, but really guilt—body-weakening guilt.

What a shit he was to act that way this morning. He would have to make it up to Sarah—as he usually had done in the past. He'd be figuratively down on his knees, begging for forgiveness, literally purchasing and presenting her with something expensive. He headed down Fortaleza Street, to the Jewels of the World emporium that occupied its own building and headed inside.

Lots of fans whirred from a high-beamed ceiling. The place was large enough for the dozens of neon-colored (clothes, skin) tourists off the liners that were docked a couple of blocks down. The air-conditioning was on full blast. In two weeks it would be Sarah's birthday. This time, would it be diamonds or gold?

"What, sir, can I do for you?" asked a short, heavy woman in a long, red flowery muumuu. She had breasts like melons.

"I'm. . uhn…just looking."

"Yes, but can I *help yo*u?"

"No, I'm just looking around."

"Of course. That's your privilege. But if you just give me a hint of what you might be looking for… ." The woman was smiling, falsely. Pablo looked at her deeply mascaraed brown eyes. There was something sad in them.

"Okay, my wife's birthday is coming up in a few weeks and I want to get some jewelry for her—maybe a necklace."

"Certainly!" said the woman. "Sergio! Sergio!" she called to a salesman behind one of the counters. "Help this man! A birthday gift for his wife."

"My pleasure," said Sergio, tall, mustachioed, a Cesar Romero look-alike. He was wearing a royal blue jacket with gold-scripted "Jewels of the World" on the breast pocket.

The woman took Pablo by the arm and steered him

toward the showcase that Romero stood smiling behind.

"What month?" Romero asked Pablo.

"Excuse me?"

"Your wife. What month was she born?"

"This month. September."

"Bueno. Sapphire."

Pablo grunted.

Romero kept grinning. "Sapphire. Her birthstone. Ring? Brooch? Necklace? Bracelet? Earrings? Matching necklace and earrings?"

"Let me see a necklace."

"Of course."

Romero opened a showcase, took out a necklace and laid it on a purple cloth that was draped over the counter. "Here is *exactly* what you want; a lavish and enchanting piece. Ten carat white gold...round diamond accents... teardrop shaped...really beautiful pear-cut sapphires. The diamonds total 1. 4 carats. The necklace, rhodium-plated, which maintains the shine, prevents tarnishing....Fourteen-point-five fantail chain..."

"How much?"

"With the special Norwegian Star discount—you are a passenger on the ship, right?"

Pablo shook his head.

"Doesn't matter," Romero said with a wink. "With that

discount, let's see, ten percent on the wholesale, twenty percent on the retail…the price, for you, $1,795. 99."

Pablo dug out his wallet and handed over his Visa card. The salesman placed the necklace in a royal blue cushioned box with the golden Jewels of the World logo scripted on the top, then swiped the Visa card through a small machine. A message came up on the screen. "Hmm," said the salesman. "Let me try again."

Another swipe and the same message. "I m sorry sir, but it says that the card is no longer…"

Pablo blinked, looked up at one of the whirring fans, then took the boxed necklace off the counter, put it in his pocket, left his credit card, which he would get fixed later—let them hold on to it—and started toward the door.

"Sir, your card, it has exp…What? Where is he going? Sir! Sir! Nestor, that man! Stop that man!"

Pablo saw out of a corner of his eye a hulking football linesman, also in a royal blue jacket with the Jewels of the World logo, stomping his way. Pablo took off through the door and was hit by the hot noon air. He caught his breath and started running down Fortaleza Street. Taking a quick look behind, he could see the royal blue jacket huffing after him.

Pablo smacked into one tourist, then another, and another, excusing himself, running into the street. He was car-beeped back onto the sidewalk, the hulk, on a walkie-talkie, pursuing.

As he reached Cristo Street, he realized the next block down was a dead end that ran into the Governor's mansion. He turned right, chugging up the hill that ran past the San Juan Cathedral and El Convento Hotel. The hulk, still trailing, still on the walkie-talkie.

Then, from the street on the side of the cathedral, two policemen appeared. He dodged past them. Whistles were blown. Tourists turned one way, then the other. More whistles, shouts, Pablo stumbling up the hill, grabbed by a cop, pushing back, hit in the head by a baton, swinging wildly, grabbed from all over, handcuffed behind his back, dragged back down to the street beside the cathedral—a gaggle of nuns standing outside with hands over their mouths—then shoved into a patrol car parked on the sidewalk, whisked away in a siren-wailing vehicle.

Incredible!

Sarah, up with Betty while Annie and Carlos still slept, was reading *El Nuevo Día* at the kitchen table while her granddaughter, who had just had her bowl of Cheerios, was on the floor, talking to and petting Blanche.

...Pablo Cruz, the artist and son of Nestor J. Cruz, the late Mayor of San Juan, Speaker of the House and losing candidate for Governor in the election of 1972, was arrested yesterday and charged with stealing a diamond necklace from the Jewels of the World Jewelry Store in Old San Juan.

After a dramatic chase along the blue-cobblestone streets of the Old City, in front of scores of frightened tourists, Cruz was finally cornered by police in front of the San Juan Cathedral and led off to the San Juan Municipal Jail.

Cruz was brought to the San Juan Judicial Center in Hato Rey for arraignment, but a fire of unknown origin in a courtroom there postponed all hearings in the building. Authorities said Cruz would be returned Monday to the judicial center.

Employees of the Jewels of the World Jewelry Store on Fortaleza Street said that Cruz ran off with the necklace after pretending to look at it as a gift for his wife, the well-known actress Sarah Figueroa. "I knew there was something suspicious about him as soon as he entered the store," said Sylvia Mason, who...

Incredible!

What should she do? She had told Annie and Carlos

that she hadn't been able to get a hold of Pablo to tell him of their visit, but had left messages for him and hoped that he would show up before they had to return, which was on Tuesday.

They were more than looking forward to their planned trip today to Dorado, where Carlos' brother, Alberto, had a beach house. Alberto had invited the whole family for a glorious Sunday with his wife and the twins (Betty's age) for swimming, sunning and a backyard cookout.

Let her daughter and family enjoy themselves, and maybe before they leave, she'll break the news. Annie is used to her father not showing up. He missed her wedding, didn't he? He couldn't get up to New York. Why? Because he couldn't get on a plane. Why? Because he couldn't.

"Pretending" to buy a necklace for her? Why else was he there, other than to get something for her after his latest fit?

Why wouldn't he listen to her and keep seeing a therapist, instead of keeping one or two appointments, then telling whomever to go fuck his/herself? If he won't do what's right for himself, how can she make him? She can't—she now knows that for sure. Only he can make a difference by helping himself.

She has to cut him off completely. Especially now, with that offer to go to Madrid to appear in the García Lorca

Festival. That Spanish producer, Carasquillo, who saw her last year in the production at the Tapia of La Casa De Bernarda Alba. He said she was the best Bernarda he had ever seen and promised he would invite her for the festival production. She thought, yeah, yeah, sure. Then, last week, the invite, by letter. Hopefully, she could make enough of a success, get more roles there, even move to Spain or maybe have a new, wider career.

So why does she feel so goddamn guilty? Oh, Je-sus! Maybe she was as screwed up as Pablo.

They sat on hard wooden, crowded benches in the basement of the Hato Rey Judicial Center, along with other relatives, friends and maybe enemies and victims of the accused, who were paraded in and out for criminal hearings in the several courtrooms there. Sarah sat along the aisle, next to a small, thin woman with gray hair in a bun who kept biting her nails and making little moaning sounds. Annie and Carlos had squeezed into the row behind her. They had left Betty with Sarah's next-door neighbor, Patricia, a schoolteacher on a sabbatical who kindly agreed to watch Betty for a few hours, along with her three pre-school children.

Sarah turned to smile at Annie. Annie nodded without smiling. Carlos was writing in his small black "things-to-do" notebook." She told them about Pablo after they had returned last night from Dorado. It had been a wonderful day. Today, she knew, would not be so wonderful.

After a one-hour wait, two cops brought Pablo in from a van that had pulled into the courtyard. Sarah motioned to her daughter and son-in-law and they followed right behind orange jump-suited Pablo.

A guard stopped them at the door to the courtroom. "This is not a public hearing," he said. "Only one relative."

"I'm his wife," said Sarah.

"Proof?"

"What are you talking about?"

"We need proof. That fire Saturday? Security has been tightened. We can't let anyone into these hearings unless they show us something that says they're a relative."

Sarah stared hard at the guard, at his slanted eyes and high-cheek-boned face. "I am Sarah Figueroa, the wife of the prisoner Pablo Cruz. I demand to be allowed in to see the proceedings against my husband!"

The guard put up a hand, turned, and went into the courtroom.

"This is incredible," Sarah told her daughter and son-in-law. They nodded.

A few minutes later, the guard returned. "One of you can enter," he said.

Sarah strode into the small courtroom and sat on a bench in the front row. She saw Pablo holding onto a rail as he stood before the judge, a stern high school principal look-alike with rimless glasses and a widow's peak that started halfway down his wide forehead. The two guards stood on each side of Pablo. The judge looked down at papers, looked at Pablo over the top of his glasses, looked back at the papers and Pablo several more times. He asked Pablo if he had contacted an attorney or a bail bondsman. Pablo shrugged. Then the judge said that Pablo was being arraigned on charges of Grand Theft and he set bail at $15,000. The judge informed Pablo that he could pay 10 percent, or $1,500 to the court, and be released until the next hearing for probable cause, which would be held within the next few weeks. If he could not post the bond, he would be returned to jail.

Pablo shrugged again. The judge frowned. "I did not agree with the politics of your father, but at least he was an honorable man. I don't understand what happened to you."

Pablo shrugged still again. The two guards grabbed his arms and were about to lead him out of the courtroom when Sarah shot up and told the judge: "Your honor, I'll pay the bail. Please don't have him returned to prison."

Who was she? the judged asked.

"I am Sarah Figueroa, the wife of Pablo Cruz."

The judge gave Sarah a hard, quizzical look. Then he broke into a small smile. "The actress? Yes, I saw you at the Tapia Theater, in Shakespeare. You were Portia. 'The quality of mercy is not strained; it drops as gentle as the rain'."

Almost.

Sarah closed her eyes, then opened them.

"Upon the place beneath. It is twice blest;

It blesseth him that gives and him that takes:

T'is mightiest in the mightiest; it becomes

The throned monarch better than his crown."

Sarah smiled up at the judge. The judge looked at Sarah with a twinkle in his eye. "If the famous actress, Miss Sarah Figueroa, gives her word that the accused will return for trail. I will release him on his own recognizance." he said.

Sarah looked over to Pablo. He shrugged.

"I will, your honor," she said. "Thank you so very much." She also gave a silent, prayerful thanks to Señor Shakespeare as she wrote out a check to free Pable—at least for a while.

Pablo mumbled his thanks to Sarah, said he would pay her back "every penny" (though the bond would be returned after the court proceedings), kissed his daughter, shook hands with his son-in-law, then said he had to go to his apartment for a few hours "to get myself into the comfort zone again." He promised he would be at Sarah's for dinner that evening.

Don't stop in any of those alcoholic unanimous "comfort

zones" on the way, thought Sarah.

Pablo hailed a cab outside the judicial center, started to get in, but stopped. He called Sarah over. She already had three twenties folded in her hand. Without him saying anything, she hugged him and gave him the bills. He blinked his thanks, turned, and got into the cab.

He still had half a bottle of Rémy Martin above the sink. He poured himself one good drink. It went down smoothly. He put the bottle back in the cabinet, crumbled onto the sofa in the living room and took a long nap. When he woke, he took a shower, turning the water hotter and hotter.

He put on khakis, a clean blue work shirt and his blue espadrilles. He went to the cabinet above the sink again. He looked at the bottle, took it and poured just an inch back into his cup. He downed it. He looked hard at the bottle. He screwed the top back on, put the bottle back on the shelf, closed the cabinet door and left the apartment.

He drank cava with the *asapao de longosta* and nursed one Felipe Segundo brandy after dinner. He was feeling... fine. On his way to Sarah's, he had stopped in Puerto Rico Drug on Plaza de Armas, the pharmacy that was like a department store, to buy a doll wearing a Puerto Rico flag dress for his granddaughter.

No one mentioned Pablo's latest "troubles" at dinner. In fact, no one said much of anything before and during dinner. They moved into the living room after, and Betty carried out her duties of kissing everyone good night. She went to bed clutching the doll. Carlos and Sarah shared the yellow-and-green-flowered sofa, and Pablo took his brandy to the Dominican rocker.

"So, how's the painting going?" Carlos asked his father-in-law.

Pablo sipped his drink. "I don't paint anymore."

Carlos looked over to Sarah. She shrugged, as though saying, "Not my fault."

Annie came back into the room. "Wow, out like a light. She was running around all day with your neighbor's kids," she told her mother, then told Pablo: "She loves that doll already, Dad. She usually doesn't get attached that quick to things."

Pablo sipped, nodded.

Carlos broke the silence, telling Pablo, "What d'ya mean, you don't paint anymore? You're an artist, you're an important artist, you're an important Puerto Rican artist."

"Yeah, who sez?"

"Anyone who knows anything about art and has seen your paintings."

"Bullshit."

"Come on, Dad," said Annie, her father-inherited sea-green eyes locked into Pablo's. "You are...what you are, which is above and beyond and deep inside, a great painter."

Pablo frowned, grumbled, then said: "I'll tell you what, how about giving me a show in your exiles gallery? I'm an exile, if there ever was one."

Daughter, wife, son-in-law exchanged bewildered, yet fearful here we-go-again glances.

Pablo said: "I'm the ultimate exile. I've been living in exile, from myself, for years.

Annie looked around, then said: "That's not bad, Dad. I think we could manage an exhibit around that. The Ultimate Exile: a retrospective—as well as new paintings."

"I'll get right on it, after my prison term."

"I'll speak to my cousin, Mike Suárez" Sarah said. "He knows the best defense lawyers on the island."

Pablo finished off his brandy. He needed another one, really bad. What he would do is go home and put his head under the pillow, but, not just yet. He poured himself another brandy.

They all watched the night's news. Pablo sipped his drink and stared at the screen. Housing project residents were staring down at the bullet-riddled bodies of two young guys killed in a gunfight between drug gangs. The people on the screen were looking at the bodies with no emotion on their faces; Pablo stared just as blankly at the scene.

The Ultimate Exile. Hey, he could live with that. He truly is an exile, alone and apart from every other human being and unto himself. So to stay true to his condition, he will stay apart. Maybe not the best arrangement in life, but not the worst.

He'll even start painting again because that will keep him apart. It'll keep him in solidarity with himself and with his thoughts, and creations.

That's as truly human as any exile could be.

He poured himself one more brandy.

Robert Friedman

Chapter 7

Bernardo greeted Carmencita, who wore an oversized, maroon-colored Harvard sweatshirt, a souvenir left by a visitor. She was carrying clean sheets from the closet to a room down the narrow hallway.

First things first: He went to the espresso machine behind the bar and drew a demitasse and toasted a sweet roll with powdered sugar. While carrying his breakfast to a table on the patio he looked toward the beach, at the morning bathers in the calm, sun-sparkling ocean.

"Tío, how's it going?" Jorge Gutierrez, Bernardo's 28-year-old "nephew," came across the patio. Bernardo gave Jorge a strong hug. At six feet, Jorge was just a couple of inches shorter than Bernardo.

Bernardo held the young man at arm's length to look at his long, thin, handsome face, shadowed by a scraggily mustache and beard. His dark brown eyes had the same fervent, questioning glint of the six-year-old Jorge who had come with an early set of foster parents to live in that slightly seedy South Beach hotel. Jorge had bonded with desk clerk-repairman Bernardo, who became "*Tío*" Bernardo, even after he went to live with Luis and Ana in Coral Gables. On Jorge's weekly visits during Bernardo's day off, he would take the boy to the beach, to a ballgame or on those rare rainy days, to the movies.

"So, you're finally back. How was it?"

"We had a great time. Yvonne was cutting cane with me and we even took Luisito out in the fields a couple of days, just so he could see what was going on."

"Any trouble getting back?"

"The usual hassle. Immigration made us wait six hours at the airport before they let us back onto the island. But they returned our passports when our lawyers showed up. After all, we're all Americans, aren't we?"

"Sure."

Jorge had become an American in 1962 at the tender age of three, one of the youngest of the more than 14,000 Operation Pedro Pan kids sent to the states by their Cuban parents. They believed what they were told by the Church, that Fidel was preparing to send Cuban kids to the Soviet Union for communist indoctrination. An aunt was to pick up Jorge and his older sister, Daniela, who was then eight, at the Miami airport. Between the time that Jorge toddled onto the

Dutch KLM jet at José Martí Airport and the plane landed at Miami International, Jorge's *Tía* Mercedes had had a fatal heart attack.

The Archdiocese of Miami stepped in and Jorge and Daniela were sent to a series of foster homes together, then separate—awaiting their parents who, while waiting for their visas, divorced, then started new families, tried to get their children back to Cuba, and then gave up the fight. Both died comparatively young, the father in Angola, the mother a suicide.

Jorge's last set of foster parents, Ana and Luis Concepción—Luis an exile, himself—adopted him and brought him to Puerto Rico at the age of nine. When Bernardo went to New York he kept in touch with Jorge through his new parents, and when Bernardo moved his family to Puerto Rico, there was a reunion. Pilar and Bernardo became close friends with Ana and Luis, and Jorge became a part of the Alvarez family, not to mention their earliest babysitter.

"Tío, this is for you." Jorge handed Bernardo a large clasped envelope. "Go ahead, open it."

Bernardo took from the envelope a dog-eared, large softcover book. He immediately recognized the building with the portal windows painted on the cover. Printed in the right corner: Belen 1959. It. was a copy of his high school yearbook.

"I know you left everything when you got out. Look at page twenty-five."

He knew what he would see: a 17-year-old with a long, thin face, a serious expression, an Errol Flynn mustache, a kid on his way to becoming—Bernardo Alvarez.

"I found it in this shop in Old Havana. They were selling all sorts of memorabilia," said Jorge.

Bernardo flipped through the pages, saw faces that began to melt his heart, then shut the book. *"Gracias, Jorgito.* This is a wonderful present." He hugged the young man then offered Jorge a cup of coffee. "You want a sweet roll?" he asked.

"No, thanks. I just ate a big breakfast." Bernardo set the coffee on a table.

"Tío, how would you feel about going back to Cuba for a visit?"

"Someday." He didn't tell Jorge that he was there most nights in his dreams. "Cuba and I aren't ready for each other yet."

"It's definitely not as bad as you may remember. I mean it's true, everything is rundown and there's rationing and everyone has to hustle to get through the day. But the people, they're still great! They're warm and welcoming and, you know…"

"Yeah, I know."

Jorge smiled somewhat sheepishly. "I'm sure you do. Well, anyway, I met some people on this trip who knew Carlos and we were talking about his assassination, and the killing in Washington of Letelier and his assistant, Roni Moffitt. And they were saying that the same people were involved in the murders, either they carried out the killings or arranged for them with the knowledge of the CIA and the FBI. I remember Carlos. We played squash together in Casa Cuba. He told me about *Areito,* how he was writing for them and asked me if I wanted to do an article for the magazine. Then, we talked about how we both were Pedro Pan kids. He was really a great guy."

Bernardo inhaled deeply, then slowly let the air out.

Looking into the coffin of a handsome young man, twenty-six, the mustache, the little beard, the damage to the forehead from the bullet touched up, almost unnoticeable. Shot down for taking part in el diálogo, *as a travel agent arranging tours for exiles going to their homeland. Shot down driving home after visiting his mother. Killer never caught. A wife, so young, a tight coat of composure willed over the roiling anguish. Two small kids holding little Cuban flags.*

"So we're going to form a group: university people, lawyers and journalists, both in Cuba and Puerto Rico. And we're going to look in-depth at the killings happening here. As you know, there were others—and maybe we'll expand the investigation to Letelier and the other murders in the states to expose the connections of the Cuban exile killers and the U. S. agencies. We want to bring all the guilty parties to justice through the World Court. Two Cuban lawyers already have spoken to people in The Hague about trying to get the court involved. So, *Tío*, what do you think?"

"I think you're playing with fire," Bernardo said.

"Just like you and my dad did before you both became...disillusioned. Dad told me his war stories in the Second Front of the Escambray, and some of yours, too. I know the scar on the side of your head was from a rifle smashed there by the militia in a demonstration against Batista. So, in my way, I'm following your examples. I know it pissed off Dad when I got to head the independence students at Central High and when I joined the movement at UPR. But I always remember what Lolita Rodriguez de Tió, the great poet, wrote: '*Cuba y Puerto Rico son de un pájaro las dos alas'.* Cuba and Puerto Rico are two wings of the same bird. And colonialism is colonialism, no matter how it's disguised, you know?"

Outside the gates of the University, he is once again face-to-face with Segundo Cruz, now a member of the Batista police force. A year before, Cruz was pitching for Colegio

Baldor when Bernardo smashed that line drive past third that knocked in the two runs that gave Colegio Belen (his school and Fidel's alma mater) the high school championship. After the game, a smile from Cruz—small, tight —the same small, tight smile that cuts into his broad, beefy face as he bashes Bernardo in the head with the butt of his rifle.

Bernardo fingered the scar from the eight stiches near his left ear. Cruz had done Bernardo a favor not shooting him as other students had been shot down on that steamy, bloody day.

Jorge continued: "I know that I really pissed off Dad when I joined the Antonio Maceo Brigade and went with them to cut sugar cane, but Cuba is where I was born. I may not belong to it now, but it belongs to me, you know? Anyway, what we're really after here, the people I met on the trip, is bringing killers to justice. You can't argue with that, can you?"

Jorge looked as though he was not sure whether Bernardo would accept the premise.

Bernardo said: "No, I can't argue with that."

Jorge smiled. *"Gracias, Tío,"* he said, as though he had just received a blessing. "We've spent so many hours talking—about everything. And I'm sure you know that I greatly respect your opinions and well. . . you know, the secular and humane things you tell me, and that I can always count on you. I know you will always be here for me, and for my family."

Bernardo nodded. Jorge took his leave.

As the day progressed, Bernardo remembered:

Asleep in the next room, he didn't even hear them when they entered, then left. He is awoken by his mother's sobbing. What happened? Where's his father?

"They took him!"

"Who took him?

"They took him for the words he wrote!"

Two days later, as Fernando Alvarez sits in a filthy prison cell, his heart stops beating. When they come for his body they are told that a Christian burial is not allowed for traitors. His mother bribes officials to find the unmarked grave, convinces an old rabbi to say prayers. Two years later the same rabbi, in the same black coat prays over the body of Bernardo's mother.

Still in high school, he joins the Llano. He runs errands, appears at protest rallies, cuts power and telephone lines. He accompanies a truck loaded with food and equipment into the Sierra Maestra and, for the first time, he sees Fidel, looking scraggily and tired. Che smiles when Bernardo greets him with a salute. In Havana, two of his friends, Juanito and Mario—who have also joined the urban underground—are beaten, killed by Batista thugs.

Castro reopens the University in 1959, after a two-year shutdown, and Bernardo becomes a freshman. An engineering degree, a builder of roads and bridges. Undoubtedly not as perceptive as his father, it takes him a while before realizing: one more dictator. As a supposed "New Man," you couldn't remain true to others, or to yourself. That was the worst, having to spend your life being other than your own true self. He is haunted by his father's death—deeply aware of how the political world has shaped and shaded the life of his parents. He owed it to them to react directly to that world. But no rationalization is needed for his escape. He is truly offended by still another forced march to make a society twist and curve and corkscrew to fit the vision of one more despotic savior.

Out the window in Mexico City.

Now, Bemardo Alvarez, age fourty-five, who lost his great love three years ago, took the days as they came. What did he want out of the rest of his life?

What did life want of him?

The next night Bernardo had a great home-cooked dinner at the home of Ana and Luis. After the *mojitos*, the creamed plantain soup, the *yuca,* the *ropa vieja* with rice and black beans, the *tres leches* and the two shots of *café cubano*, he walked Anita and Carlos home and made sure they got to bed. Then he returned to his friends' house.

Jorge and his wife, Yvonne, and their little Luisito, age three, had also been at the dinner. While Bernardo's kids were at the table, the talk had been about old friends and old places in Cuba, and not about politics. But once Bernardo had returned after bringing his children home, Yvonne put Luisito to bed upstairs, and Mauricio and Celia Pérez dropped by for a drink. The political "discussion" became unavoidable.

The Pérezes had come from a hotel banquet where meat importer Mauricio was being honored by the local chapter of the Cuban-American National Foundation as Businessman of the Year. Among other things, he had been cited for his ban on bringing Nicaraguan beef onto the island.

Tall and lean, with refined features and a low-keyed voice, he confounded almost everyone when they learned of his background as a "butcher" in Cuba. Actually, he had inherited a meat processing plant in Havana from his father, who had become wealthy catering to the exclusive hotels and richest families by purchasing the choicest cuts from Argentina, Uruguay and the United States. Before taking over the business, Mauricio Pérez had earned degrees at the University of Havana and the Wharton School of the University of Pennsylvania. He was in his early fifties and had been in exile for some 20 years; he still hated everything about the revolution.

Ana and Luis had more or less forgotten that Mauricio and Celia would be dropping by for a drink, which they now realized could turn awkward, given the recent return of their son and his family from a friendly visit to Cuba. But Jorge had returned from the trip earlier than expected and the Pérezes couldn't be disinvited at the last minute. So now the men were in the parlor drinking Gran Marnier and B&B while Celia Pérez and Yvonne helped Ana clean up.

After pleasantries about families and friends—Mauricio told of how the twins were following in his footsteps, enrolled at the Wharton School at the University of Pennsylvania—he then got right to it. His eyes opening wide, as though in anticipated surprise, he said to Jorge: "Jorge, *m'ijo,* tell us about your trip to the land that time forgot. Will they meet the projected sugar harvest this year? Are the people still fighting for the meat that appears in the market once every blue moon, like dogs battling over scraps?"

Actually, Jorge did know some figures on the harvest— a figure that was approaching eight million metric tons—but was sure that his father's friend couldn't care less.

"Economically, times are tough, as usual," Jorge said. "But the people remain hopeful."

"Oh, really? What people are those? The Soviet people, who have become the new imperialists in the homeland? The government of Marxist-Communist bureaucrats? Fidel and

Raul? The people. Are you sure?"

Jorge took a deep breath. He had been in the company of Mauricio Pérez twice before when Pérez had visited his father, but had remained silent as the two older men tore down the revolution.

"It's true, the people do continue to suffer," Jorge said, seeming to offer a consoling answer. "But their suffering is not of their own doing. They know deep down that they have taken the right path and that life will get better. Actually, it is already better for many who had been held back before Fidel. The education is tremendous and the health services..."

Bernardo tried to blink away, then drink away, the rest of the conversation as it became more heated and less reasonable. He had heard it all before: *El Bloqueo,* the stupid and reactionary policy of Washington; the egotism and selfishness of the exiles in Miami; the fear of Cuba's "New Man."

"I understand you are giving a talk next week at the University about Cuba," said Pérez, who, like all exiles connected to *La Lucha,* the fight against Castro, and knew of every scheduled event for or against the current Cuban regime.

"You are a young man who has never lived in the land, except as a baby. You have absolutely no first-hand knowledge of the dictatorship," said Pérez. "You've been there for a couple of weeks and were fed the usual propaganda for visitors. You see schools and hospitals, but never the prisons packed with the *real* patriots of Cuba. So, my question is this: What gives *you* the right to pass judgment on *my* country, the country where I was born and grew up and where, as a young man, my values and habits were formed, where I met and fell in love with my wife, where my children were created, where my parents and their parents and their parents' parents are buried, all in my once bright and wonderful and lovable, now darkly depressed and cruelly oppressed country. What gives you that right?"

"As long as I was born there, it's my country, too," said Jorge, looking around for confirmation and getting a nod from Bernardo.

Pérez threw his head back and laughed. "He left Cuba at what—two? Three? And he considers himself a *guajiro!*"

"I consider myself as Cuban as...as anyone. I didn't choose to leave."

"Then why don't you go back to live there?"

"Well, I..."

"Well...well...you are like every other Castro lover who lives somewhere else and spreads the lies and the *mierda* of that *cabrón* so that he remains in power when a machete should be put to his neck and his head should be chopped off and hung on a pole in Plaza Civica."

Pérez finished his drink, pulled himself out of the easy chair and went to a sideboard bar to refill his glass. He held up a bottle of Johnny Walker Black. "May I, Don Luis?"

"Of course. *Mi casa es su casa.*"

Pérez poured a generous amount into his glass, dropped a few ice cubes into his drink and returned to the easy chair. He stared into the drink before downing half of it, then looked up again at Jorge, addressing him in a studied calmness. "I ask you, as the...the dependent...of one of my best friends, to postpone your lecture at the University. No more lies about that *sinvergüenza.* No more uninformed criticism against the United States for its policy against the atheistic, God-hating Havana dictatorship." He drank, mumbled to himself, then nodded, as though deciding that what he would say next would be the crushing blow against the ungrateful adopted son of a good friend.

"And may I add, instead of standing in front of other easily swayed young people and feeding them with revolutionary garbage, you should be down on your knees giving thanks that you have been able to escape the misery of living in today's Cuba. Thanks to *this man"*—he looked over and pointed a finger at Luis Concepción— "excuse me, Don Luis, but it is time someone points this out."

Don Luis closed his eyes and shook his head in a kind of false modesty.

Jorge, looking down to the black-and-white terrazzo floor and started: "I appreciate and I understand all that has been done for me, but..."

"But, but..." Pérez said disdainfully. "But, but..."

"I have a right to share with others..."

"You have no right to spread communist lies!"

Then Bernardo said: "All right. Enough."

Pérez shot a look at Bernardo. "What? Enough? Enough of what? Enough of this young man's lies?"

"Enough of your bullying. Cut it out!" Something clicked inside Bernardo, setting off a tingling of nerves.

Pérez finished his drink, went to the sideboard and filled up his glass again, careful not to spill the liquid over the top. Then he turned to Bernardo. His jaw moved from side to side.

"We know all about you, too. We know from friends in Miami about your traitorous behavior toward plans for another invasion. We know that you then fled Miami, and that those plans had to be postponed because of the belief of many that you were, at the very least, an agent for those so-called liberals in Washington who opposed freeing the Cuban people from tyranny. We know that you are always running and have no principles when it comes to overthrowing the world's worst dictator. Yes, we know you're not even Cuban-born! What, then, are you?"

Bernardo's head went light. He got up and walked over to Pérez, standing no more than an inch from him. "Who the hell do you think you are?" he said.

"I know who *I* am," Pérez said. "And I know what *you* are: a goddamn lying coward!"

Pérez threw his drink in Bernardo's face. Bernardo reached back and slapped Pérez hard, just below the eye.

The slap seemed to sting the other occupants of the room; they put their hands to their cheeks. Mauricio Pérez bent his head down, as though in embarrassment. Then he rammed it into Bernardo's chest. Bernardo and Pérez tumbled together across a coffee table that held a picture book of Old Havana. The table broke in half. Bernardo was pushing both hands under Pérez's chin, while Pérez was trying to kick Bernardo. Their legs became entwined.

Jorge kept shaking his head, saying, "No, no, no," while Luis Concepción shot up from his chair, but stood motionless. The women ran into the room from the kitchen, then froze alongside Luis Concepción, covering their mouths. Finally, Luis and Jorge jumped in and pulled Bernardo and Pérez apart. Bernardo and the others got to their feet. The large parlor reverberated with silence.

Everyone stood around, breathing heavily and deeply embarrassed.

"I'm extremely sorry that I lost my head," Bernardo told

his hosts.

Other apologies followed. Then Ana Concepción went to the piano in a front corner of the room. With her back to everyone, she began playing the Cuban classic, *Siboney.*

Back at the guesthouse, Bernardo had one more brandy before going to bed. The last customers had left the bar and Perry was washing out glasses.

"How was your night?" Perry asked.

"Like old times," said Bernardo. Perry nodded. They exchanged half-sympathetic, half-sardonic smiles.

Bernardo suddenly flinched as he saw, in his mind's eye, his father dying in the prison cell.

He drank as the sea softly crashed against the shore.

Robert Friedman

Chapter 8

When Marta Silva and Don Cisco extended their neighborhood walks from occasional Sunday mornings to weekday evenings, Marta confessed to herself, if to no one else, that she couldn't wait to return from her job behind the perfume counter at the González Padín Department Store. The evening walks were filled with Don Cisco retelling stories he'd read and what they meant to him, and his thoughts, feelings and opinions about life. Marta knew that much of what Don Cisco said was for his own benefit, as he reaffirmed lessons he had learned, both through books and through his eighty-three summers and occasional winters in New York where he had lived—he told Marta with a slight shiver—with the first of his three wives. Marta was not sure whether the quiver represented the weather or the marriage, or both.

Marta lived down the hall from Don Cisco on the second

floor of the Solimar Guesthouse. The one large room had been turned into two with an arched wall separating the living quarters and a kitchenette. There was a small bathroom with a shower stall across from the kitchenette. She had been there for the past three years, after the death of her mother, with whom she had always lived, except for the one year she had spent at university in Madrid. She began studying languages there with the goal of becoming a translator, perhaps at the United Nations. But she soon became very interested in art history and even took drawing and painting classes. She spent hours at the Prado Museum, always lingering in front of the Velázquez paintings. She continually studied Las Meninas—the painter painting himself painting; that lovely little golden-haired girl; the face of that dwarf. She had to cut short her stay abroad and her education when her father, a pharmacist, died of a heart attack. As an only child, she understood she had to come home to care for her mother, a jobless housewife.

Marta, now sixty-seven and never married, had seldom dated in her younger years. She was small, thin, shy and, she understood, not very attractive. She had a rectangular face; large, dark sad eyes; pale lips and lifeless brown hair. One lukewarm love affair was all she had had in her adult life, more than 30 years ago, with a man who at the time had recently left the priesthood. After a while, he confessed to her that his true attraction was to young men, but that they should remain friends, which they did until he left the island some years later to live in his native Argentina.

In the past few years, she spent many hours cutting and tearing stories and photos from newspapers and magazines, as well as using photos of her youth and of her own abstract and figurative paintings, along with all sorts of cloth materials and flowers, small stones, buttons, little objects she had picked up in the street to paste them into collages. Putting these things together, feeling their textures, seeing how they complemented and contrasted with one another gave her a deep feeling of satisfaction. Her collages were all over her rooms, hung on the walls and leaning against walls, cabinets, dressers. The few visitors she had, mostly relatives, usually either ignored them or grudgingly nodded at their existence— except for Don Cisco. The first time he entered Marta's rooms—she had invited him in for lemonade one evening after their walk—he closely inspected the collages. They were "truly wonderful," he said, "combining the surreality of our dreams and the longing in our everyday lives."

Their friendship had begun one night when Don Cisco knocked on Marta's door. The lights in the guesthouse and the neighborhood had gone out. Did Miss Silva have a spare candle? She offered him two thick, red prayer candles with "Santa Barbara" sketched in white on the glass enclosures, telling him she had several more for such emergencies. Early the next morning, a Sunday, Don Cisco returned the still-usable candles and asked if he could have the pleasure of her company for a walk in the now partially sunny, cooled-off streets. Miss Silva agreed.

For their first walk, Don Cisco was dressed in a white guayabera, sharply creased dark slacks and shiny black loafers. The brim of his Panama hat was snapped down on his flat forehead. Miss Silva had on a plain yellow dress, large white plastic-rimmed sunglasses, green sandals and a floppy straw hat. The walk, like those that followed on several Sundays, took them down Ashford Avenue, past the ocean front tourist hotels and high-rises, all the way to the Dos Hermanos Bridge, which spanned the Condado Lagoon. Before returning to the guesthouse, they always stopped for iced tea in the shaded terrace restaurant of the Condado Plaza Hotel.

During those walks and "tea times," Don Cisco seldom stopped talking. He covered just about all topics, from art ("The great portraits give me the most satisfaction as they depict the thoughts and emotions of their subjects in the deepest human terms"), to literature ("All of life and culture are on the pages in the novels of Mr. Dickens and Monsieur Balzac"), to politics ("Why is it that politicians never seem to address the real problems of the people?"), to religion ("I truly wish I could believe in God, but I cannot accept anything on faith alone") and love ("There is no true love without true sacrifice").

Although Don Cisco's scientific and realistic views were in the forefront—he was a retired high school biology teacher—he did not completely dismiss the idea of reincarnation. He believed, he often said, in no final explanation of anything, especially why there is life, whether there is God, what will happen after death. Marta agreed, more or less (it was as difficult for her to say there was no God, or to positively affirm His existence).

The only lines on Don Cisco's darkest brown skin (he traced his roots to Mozambique) occurred in crinkles around his eyes when he smiled. When in the company of others, the smile seemed perpetual.

When he wasn't reading, Don Cisco was writing. He often read to Marta the letters he had written and received from his five children who lived in several places around the world: an Air Force captain son in Germany, a pediatrician daughter in California, a policeman son in Chicago, a teacher daughter in New York and another teacher daughter in Kenya. He had written a memoir, which he confessed to Marta was less than fair to his three wives, two of whom he left while the other one, Jamaican-born, told him *"adiós."* Number three had left him, he said, because she said she loved him too much and knew that because he had so many other interests, he could never return her feelings. She was, said Don Cisco, a strange woman who claimed to have psychic powers, which of course, was ridiculous. From time to time, she would phone him to let him know where his life would be going.

Well, he was now writing a novel about love among the elderly at a retirement home. He read his daily output to Marta. The first chapter of the novel related how two neighbors, both with incipient memory loss, begin to fall in love with each other, their still strongly felt emotions overwhelming all memory lapses.

"Face, name, personal traits of the other faded after each meeting," Don Cisco read. "But the deep, terrifying, poignant pain of first love renewed itself upon each subsequent encounter."

He told Marta that the couple will live together in a senior citizens community; then the woman will develop dementia, then Alzheimer's, then will have to be moved to a special care home, where she will live on with no memory. One month after the woman is taken from their home, the man will die of a broken heart.

Marta said little during Don Cisco's readings and his pronouncements. Mostly she just smiled and nodded. She had seldom met such an intelligent, well-read man with opinions she either agreed with or was willing to accept because of the knowledge behind them and the way he expressed them. Her own comments, she felt, would add little if anything, to the one-way "conversation." Don Cisco seldom asked for her input, except one Sunday when he had made his proclamation on love.

"Do you agree that sacrifice is a requisite of any love affair?" he asked, raising eyebrows so thin, they could have been penciled in. He drew through a straw a steady stream of iced tea from a tall glass while smiling with his black eyes.

"I believe sacrifice in love means that you, I, the person who deeply loves another, would be willing to...rather, it would be natural for that person because of his or her deep feelings, to do what or to give up, that which the loved one desires." Marta felt her thin-boned face turning red.

"Yes," said Don Cisco softly, reaching out to touch her hand resting on the table. He tapped her fingers lightly twice and flashed his bright white dentures.

Both sipped their iced teas through straws.

The idea came to Marta as she woke the next morning. She wanted to begin painting again.

When she had to return to Puerto Rico from Madrid, during that first year she had done some paintings—beach scenes, scenes of the countryside, *jíbaros* working in the fields. Mostly watercolors. She wanted to paint again, this time with oils, a medium she hadn't used since her student days but realized she had to use now. She wanted to paint a portrait of Don Cisco to show him through the picture what was so difficult for her to express in words.

She felt very close to him. The feeling was like a distant memory, something she knew she had felt so seldom in her old-maid's life. A sad life, she had accepted for so many years. If she were looking at another life like her own, she would think: what a pity! So many years!

Bueno, now she would reach out. Now, after so many years of sadness, she would reach out to Don Cisco by painting his portrait.

Marta sits in front of a blank canvas. Don Cisco sits on a straw-backed chair across from her. She stares hard at Don Cisco and he smiles, but looks somewhat frightened, which she realizes, is the last emotion she would have expected to see on his creased, burnt-umber face.

"Please, Don Cisco, I want to paint you to…to…show you, show me, show the world…"

She will outline his head. No, she will start with the eyes. She studies the blackness of the iris, the yellowed sclera, the very bulging cornea. She tips her thinnest brush, a double 0, onto the palette, applies the oil onto the canvas and…and nothing happens! She picks up a number 2 brush, goes into the palette, onto the canvas and…still nothing!

She switches to charcoal for a simple line drawing. She

will apply the paint later. She starts on the head.

Still, nothing.

She reapplies gesso onto the canvas, one then two coats, then sands the canvas lightly, then starts drawing the head again in oil, a very thinned-out burnt sienna, a number two, then a number four brush again, then wider and wider brushes, more deeply dipped into the paint, soaked, scrubbed, swirled onto the canvas.

Nothing. Nothing!

Why? She tries again and again, but the canvas remains white, white and blank. Her breath comes short. She begins to cry. She looks at Don Cisco. He is turned half away. His bushy mustache below his long straight nose twirls up his cheek. His straight black hair is neck-length. His eyes are dark, impenetrable. A frown is forming on his face. She puts out a hand hoping he will tap her fingers, before she realizes, suddenly and with a deep plunging in her bowels, that it is not Don Cisco sitting there. It is Diego Velazquez, the great painter, who now unmistakably frowns, then turns his face from her.

Feeling the tears behind her eyes, Marta pulled herself from the bed and padded across the room to the old-fashioned roll top desk she had bought at the Salvation Army store. She pulled up the roll top and picked up her brown leather dream diary. Several other expensive leather-covered journals filled with her dreams were piled in two corners of the desk. She took a ballpoint from a brown leather cup—like the journals, bought at a discount at the González Padin stationary department. Then she returned to her bed, propped herself up on two pillows, and entered her latest dream in the diary.

She wrote: "The more I struggled the more I could not form an image of Don Cisco on the canvas, which has two meanings. One, I really do not have a full picture of the man in my mind, and two, I have so little confidence in myself to be able to reach out to him in a way he will reciprocate.

"But these premises, while deep within me, could be false. How much previous knowledge must the artist have of a particular subject before executing through shape, shadows, lines, forms, the contours of the face, which if captured truthfully would have to, at the least delineate, or at the most, signify the inner person? Perhaps it is just a matter of my fear that I lack the skill to render Don Cisco in the chosen medium? But why Velazquez sitting in place of Don Cisco? Because the artist, all those artists serious about their work, doubt that I will ever achieve a work of any value.

"And if that is the sentiment, I will challenge it. I will convince Don Cisco to sit for a portrait and I will paint it in oil, and I will capture his spirit and his soul!"

She showered, dressed, prepared for one more day at the department store perfume counter. On week nights after work, she would knock on Don Cisco's door and make the portrait proposal to him.

On Sunday, Don Cisco sat on the cane-backed chair in the center of Marta's work-living dining room. He wore a long-sleeved white guayabera buttoned at the cuffs and an eager smile on his dark brown face. His black pupils appeared to gleam in the natural light coming through the four fully opened Miami windows. Marta Silva was working in charcoal, sketching the somewhat flat shape of Don Cisco's head, which was tilted upward. She marked off the distance between the top of the forehead and the eyes, the position of the eyes, the flat nose, the bottom of the strong and just a bit jowly chin.

Don Cisco had been more than agreeable to have his portrait painted. He said he was flattered and certainly curious how Marta would portray him on the canvas. Would she, he thought, be able to capture his, well, his intelligence and his willingness to accept the world and the people who inhabit it for what it and they are? *We shall see*, thought Don Cisco.

Marta thought burnt umber and Van Dyke brown. She thought shape, shadow, lines. As the painting progressed, Marta postponed just about all their walks for the time being. On week, nights after work, she would go to the Carnegie Library to see what she could learn about portrait painting.

"The art of portraiture approached its apex during the

sixteenth century in Europe with the discovery of oil painting when the old masters developed and refined techniques that remain unsurpassed to this day. The ascendance of nonrepresentational art in the middle of the twentieth century displaced these venerable skills, especially in academic art circles..."

How would she paint Don Cisco? Realistically, impressionistically, expressionistically, abstractly? Whatever it took to capture the essence of his being.

Representational, of course. The essence of his being through the reality of precisely rendered eyes, mouth, expression, creases, cracks, blemishes... .

On Saturdays, Don Cisco tutored students having trouble with biology and the sciences. On Sundays, he posed. He started sitting for the portrait three or even five hours at a time, mostly in good humor and as usual, relating what he had learned about the world from recent readings and observations. Marta barely listened and at times told him to please stop talking, keep his head at an upward angle and hold still as she concentrated on a facial feature. Don Cisco of course complied, but soon cut the sittings to fewer hours, then to about an hour, claiming that the sessions were turning out more tiring than if he had spent the time running around a track.

Marta continually corrected what she had earlier painted

and found she did not have all the proper materials. She needed fine sable brushes, Filbert bristles and just the right colors—certainly a dioxazine purple to mix with the burnt umber for the skin tone. Also, some raw umber, a yellow green, a cobalt blue and some sort of scarlet. Well, she was learning.

Don Cisco excused himself from the next scheduled Sunday sitting. He was feeling ill; stomach pains that reoccurred from time to time. He knew if he rested in bed for the day and ate little, they would disappear and he would be his usual self the next day. While resting, he would continue writing his novel, which he had laid aside too many weeks ago. Marta, he said, would appreciate a silly dream he had some nights ago. He dreamt he had completed the novel, that it was a great success and he had won awards.

Marta suggested that they spend some time on the painting during the week after she returned from work. Don Cisco agreed. But on the evening scheduled for the sitting, he embarrassingly announced that his stomach pains had not completely disappeared and were now accompanied by strange fluctuations in his chest. Yes, he intended to make an appointment with the doctor, though he really was not too worried. "I know my body," he told Marta. "I'm sure this is just a temporary upset that will soon disappear."

Marta worked on the painting in his absence.

The background: make it simple, contrasting to the basic skin tone, a dark umber mixed with a little rose. A little shadow from the head, based on the direction of the light in the portrait. Learning. Learning. Well along. Just another sitting or two, to perfect the soul's mirror: the shape of the socket, the angles and thickness of brow, the relationship of brow to eye, line of eye, curve of lids, the fold, line, lashes, wrinkles and, of course, the color of the pupils. Neat black, yes, yet those silvery pinpoints that spark an essence of being. Yes, she will depict the soul of Don Cisco through color, lines, form.

Don Cisco tried to resume the sittings, but after just fifteen or twenty minutes, found that he could not continue to pose. Various pains and dizziness overtook him. He told Marta he liked the portrait so far (though, just a few minor points: the image he saw daily in his mirror, he said with a laugh and a wink, seemed a bit more handsome, compassionate, assured and intelligent). But, more seriously now, somehow the act of silent posing stirred a violent reaction in his body and his head.

Marta looked deeply into Don Cisco's eyes. She saw through the silvery pinpoints, to the true essence of Don Cisco; she saw what made him a humane individual; but she also saw what made him merely human, and when she saw all that, she realized that she would spend the rest of her life painting.

"That's fine," she told Don Cisco. "I don't need you here anymore. Give me another hour at the canvas, then let us resume our walks."

Robert Friedman

Chapter 9

Stumbling down Ashford, Paco lit up a Camel. He convinced himself that he didn't give a good goddamn if he ever went back to that shithole of a bar again. Crazy guys talking to themselves, *"gusanos"* probably secretly working for Castro. From now on, he'd do the high-class tourist hotels only. The drinks cost more but you meet a better class of alcoholic there. Kid the tourists. Let them know he fought in Nam—for them. American to American. Cage some drinks.

He made it to the Sheraton, the hi-rise Godzilla right there on the beach. The lobby was smooth and cool. A hooker lounging in a stuffed leather chair gave him the deep eye. Nice plump lips. Probably just serviced some tourist who earlier in the day took it up the *culo* from some AIDS-riddled *pato* he'd met on the beach. Who the fuck knew anymore who was doing what with who? The whole sex scene here was fucked up.

The bar was next to the casino. Three or four couples

and one guy on his own. He checked his watch. Half-past midnight. He'd sit next to the guy, who was wearing a black-and-green shirt with parrots on it. He'd switch from all those friggin beers to a classy scotch.

"Gimme a Cutty Sark on the rocks," he told the bartender. He lit another Camel, inhaled, knocked down the scotch, ordered another, then said to the guy: "I see you got a thing for parrots."

The guy smiled. Blond hair, blue eyes, good tan, some wrinkles, could be in his mid-forties, early-fifties.

"Yup, I do," the guy said. "Especially the *Amazona vittata.*"

"No shit," said Paco.

The guy kept smiling, winked, put out his hand. "Fred Harris of U. S. Fish and Wildlife."

"Frank Market," said Paco, who always translated Francisco Mercado when he introduced himself to gringos. "Of too many places, including Khe Sanh, Nam Dong and Têt."

The guy nodded slowly, seeming to confirm what he had known as soon as Paco sat next to him. "Vietnam vet. I missed it. Too old."

So he was in his fifties. Didn't look it. "What you missed was killing to defend the American way of life."

The guy creased up his face, then decided Paco was

being sarcastic. "Well, I'll have to settle for defending the Puerto Rican parrot's way of life," he said, flashing white teeth, like he was turning on his brights.

"Yeah?"

"I'm down from Washington to see how the Recovery Plan is doing at the aviary in El Yunque. We're concentrating right now on captive breeding."

"Yeah, I read something about it in the papers. Like there were about ten of the birds left in the whole world." Paco coughed—the fuckin' cigarettes—and lit up another one.

"A little, but not much, more than that. You know, there were about a million of them when Columbus came to the island."

"So they got killed off, like the Indians, right? That's what life is all about. Kill or be killed."

The guy blinked away Paco's statement. "We're slowly increasing the population, chicks are hatching and we're trapping the black rat predators. We're even releasing some into the wild. We're going to save those beautiful little birds!" His mouth got tight. Then he smiled again. He downed whatever he was drinking and ordered another.

"So, I'll tell you what I think," said Paco. "I think Puerto Rico would be a great place to live, if it wasn't for the goddamn Puerto Ricans!"

The guy pulled his head back and put his hands out,

palms up. "What? Who said anything…?"

Paco winked at the guy, puffed his cigarette down, squished it in a hotel logo ashtray, and for the first time, smiled a nicotine-toothed smile. "Hey, just kiddin'. That's what the gringo tourists usually say, right?"

"I don't know any…"

"Yeah. Hey, let me tell you about Nam. I was a tunnel rat and we burned down the hooches and whoever was in them, tough shit. And we napalmed the food in the fields, and I, personally, slit lots of throats. You get down in the tunnels there and sneak up when the gooks are snoozing and you slash with your Mark II from ear-to fuckin'-ear and they open their eyes, like what's waking me in the middle of my beautiful dream? Then they see the blood spurting and they give you a look like, 'What the fuck?' It's pretty fuckin' funny. It's sad, but it's funny, too. That was war, man. Kill or be killed."

The guy had his head down practically in his drink.

"I did it for us," said Paco. "For the United States of America, of which Puerto Rico is as much a part of as Witchi-what-the-fuck, Kansas." That usually got an uncomfortable laugh. This guy wasn't laughing.

Another topic. "So what about AIDS?" said Paco.

"What about it?" The friggin guy was actually getting angry. Defensive? Was he a queer?

"It's God's revenge on the homos," said Paco. "If the homos take over, we're gonna become like the Puerto Rican parrot."

The guy took a deep breath, let the air out, and looked around like he was searching for the nearest exit.

"Hey, listen," said Paco "I just spent the last dollar from my VA disability check. You think you could buy me a drink?"

The guy called over the bartender, told him to refill Paco's drink, threw some bills on the bar and without saying anything, took off.

Funny how people react to his spiel. Some laugh along, make believe they're buddy-buddy. This guy couldn't, or wouldn't, fake it. He got the free drink anyway.

He downed the scotch and got up from the bar. The hooker was still sitting in the leather chair, tapping a toe on the maroon carpet. Paco winked at her. She moved forward in the chair, about to stand. Paco waved her back down. He left the air-conditioned lobby and took off down humid Ashford Avenue again. Salsa was booming from the passing cars, hookers were eyeing tourists and shooting the shit with cops on the beat. Live and let live. *Viernes social,* social Friday, in San Juan.

Next stop, the Condado Beach Hotel, the first luxury spot built for the tourists. He did what he always did when he first arrived there, went down to the part of the lobby with the photos on the walls of the early visitors: Cornelius Vanderbilt III, the trillionaire's grandson who put up the place in 1919; Theodore Roosevelt Jr. , President Teddy's son, who also happened to have been a governor of Puerto Rico— Paco knew his U. S. -P. R. history—Lindbergh; Errol Flynn; Bob Hope; Ruebenstein the piano player; FDR and the wife.

Past one o'clock and the lounge-bar was still packed. A combo was blasting out a merengue and the dance floor was filled. Lots of locals, all dressed to the nines. Too crowded for Paco. He pushed his way out.

His goddamn feet were beginning to hurt, since they were dragging two hundred and fifty pounds around, and he was getting winded. Fucked up metabolism and hormones and genes, along with the crap he ate and, of course, the friggin' cigs. But the last place he wanted to go was "home," to the one crappy room in the latest boarding house.

When they finally stopped his treatment at the VA hospital in Río Piedras, he decided to stay in the neighborhood. How many goddamn years had he been in and out of there? He hoped to hell that he didn't have to go in again. But you never could tell. Twenty-two days in Nam, one battle, and he cracked. Never even fired his rifle. He went fuckin'…crazy. Only thing he wanted to kill was himself. Why? Why not? He never completely found out. The Army shrinks said he did not like himself. So who the fuck likes themselves? Had to learn to live with. . . whatever. Now he was… what? Cured? No family, so he lived in one boarding house after another. Construction jobs here and there and just enough in his disability check to get through the month. What kept him going were his nights in the bars around town, acting out the war hero, the macho disgust of *maricones*. He was a goddamn actor. "Playing" these parts, talking death every night, that was what kept him going. He should go into show biz. There was still time. Still, part of him hated himself for his bullshit performances. Did real actors feel that way? Were they nuts too?

He took a taxi to the Caribe Hilton. The taxi door was opened by a hotel worker. He loved this place. The flamingos and peacocks roaming the grounds, the white sandy beach, the huge windows surrounding the Oasis Bar giving views of the ocean and the palm trees. The Puerto Rico he always bragged about to his Army buddies before he…cracked.

He caught a sign in the lobby welcoming the American Bar Association to its yearly convention. The bar here also was packed—with asshole laywers.

He started a conversation with two guys at the bar, both lawyers from New York. They heard him out on his Vietnam bullshit, slashing and burning through the hooches and tunnels, and his rant about the goddamn fairies killing off everybody with their fuckin' AIDS. Then they began cross-examination.

"Why were you cutting throats in Vietnam? Were you under orders, or did you take it on yourself to act like a barbarian? Since we now understand that America's role in Vietnam was unnecessary, unjust and immoral, shouldn't you be considered a war criminal?

"And your attitude toward victims of AIDS? Where's your compassion for your fellow man, regardless of his sexual inclination? Suppose a certain disease began to spread among Puerto Ricans. Would you condemn them all?"

"Hey, I'm not a Puerto Rican," said Paco. "I mean, I am, but I'm also, mostly, a *fuckin'* American!"

The two lawyers—one in his sixties, the other in his thirties, both with high foreheads and large, balding heads, thin-rimmed glasses, blubbery lips, they looked like father and son—gave each other shit-eating grins. Paco spread his lips ear-to-ear and winked at them. He lit another Camel.

"Fuck you both," he said, deciding he didn't want those assholes buying him a drink.

Another taxi, this one to the Old City. He was running low on cash. He would sleep at a bar, or in a storefront until the Río Piedras buses began running steady in the morning.

First stop, the Mundomalo, where the dregs did their drinking. Like the guy sitting at a table next to the jukebox nursing a beer. They called the guy "Overcoat" because he always wore a gray overcoat down to his ankles, even on scorching days. His face was as gray as his coat, which was stained from all the soup kitchens on the island. He kept standing, then sitting down, standing and sitting.

Paco took a seat at the bar. In a couple of minutes, a *loca* took a seat next to him. The guy-girl tapped the back of his/her puffy red-haired wig and pouted crimson-colored lips at Paco, who was about to tell him/her where to go when another crazy came by and the two of them went, arm in arm, giggling out of the bar.

Then Paco got into a phony argument with some guy with a curly mustache and fake British accent, wearing a pith helmet. The man claimed Puerto Rico would have been so much better off if the island had been conquered by the British and had become part of the the world's greatest empire. "We have always known how to treat our bloody wogs," said the flabby face beneath the pith helmet.

When Paco told the guy to go fuck himself, pith helmet winked and said: "I'll drink to that." He bought himself, Paco and a few others at the bar several rounds. "Put it on my chit," he kept telling the bartender, who complied.

Paco spun out of the bar at, according to his Timex, twenty minutes after three. Somewhere in the back of the numbness of his mind, he felt a mounting depression. He didn't get a chance in these last hours to address that which was always foremost in his mind: death and sex. Death by war and sex with…whoever. Life, Paco knew, was a fuckin' farce. A dead-serious fuckin' farce.

He fought the urge to collapse in a door front and take a nap. He lit a Camel. He coughed up phlegm. He walked as straight up as he could under the arches in front of City Hall, then down San Francisco

The *loca* in the bar, reminded him of Marty. The eyes were all made up, but deep in the brown was Marty.

How the hell did Marty get into the army? You could tell how he was by the way he said everything, with his eyes.

That day in the shower, Marty giving him a blow job. It was nice. It was more than nice. He came forever. Which didn't in any way make him, himself, queer—no way. A blow job is a blow job. You take it where or when or from who you can. He heard later that Marty was blowing lots of guys, which didn't make them queer either. Still, the news, somehow, saddened Paco.

He reached the Plaza Colón, where he would get a bus out to Río Piedras, whenever the hell the bus would come along. A couple of bums were lying on benches. He gave in and collapsed on a bench, clasping his hands behind his head. Overhead on a high column, holding a flag—of Spain?—was ol' Christopher Columbus, who started the whole goddamn

America thing (not counting the Indians). A water fountain gurgled and very soon Paco thought he heard himself snoring.

He shot up, looked around. He rested his head back on his hands again.

That goddamn faggot Marty had invaded his head, in a barely remembered dream, and now in the groggy waking.

Basic training again and Marty helped him finish one of those overnight marches by switching boots during a break because Paco's boots were too small and crushing his toes. Did that really happen, or did he just dream it?

When he got a crush on that little blonde with the southern drawl at the Fort Campbell PX, Marty helped him write a poem to her. He gave it to her as she was ringing up his cigs, beer and other items. After he paid, she looked at the poem, scrunched up her nose and looked funny at Paco and told him she was sorry but she was engaged, and that was that.

When he left for Nam as an infantryman Marty stayed in the states, a supply clerk. He told Paco to take care of himself. Marty gave him a St. Christopher medal, which he said his mother had given him for protection. They embraced. There were tears in Marty's eyes. He felt sad himself.

Marty was one good guy. A good friend. Paco missed him. He felt the tears welling. He turned on his side, his head on his folded hands.

The little blonde with the southern drawl smiles at him and takes his hand. "What beautiful writing!" she says. Marty slaps him on the back. He goes off to war, comes back a hero, the girl is waiting for him. She's got Marty's eyes. They kiss deep. A warm tingle wells up inside him.

He winks at Marty who winks back.

Chapter 10

"Puerto Rico as the hemispheric bridge to a new value system for the Western World." That was the dream then. That remains the dream.

Edwig Messinger still believed in a humanistic future as mankind's best chance at survival. After realizing he could no longer afford his studio apartment in the luxury condominium on Ashford Avenue across from the Sheraton Hotel, he did what had to be done. He told the owners from whom he leased the apartment that he would be moving at the end of the month; spent an exhausting day searching for a new place to live. But he refused to leave the beach area, where he had started out so many years ago. So he looked at guesthouses for a temporary stay before he found an apartment he could afford. A week ago, he came upon the Solimar Guesthouse in Ocean Park, not that far from the condo he would be leaving in a week and a half. It seemed the best place for a hopefully short stay.

He was at the guesthouse bar, as he had been for the past few evenings, slowly sipping a beer before he returned to the apartment. The bartender, his name was Perry, seemed an amiable fellow who took the stories Edwig had begun to tell him with the proper sympathy and seriousness.

Edwig reminded himself once more how ahead of his time he had been, still was. He had been a visionary with property who had wanted more than anything to develop both the property and his vision—link them together for the greater good—until...until the bastards took the property from him. The Harold K. Morrow Investment Company, based in Santa Monica, California, had informed him that since he had missed the third payment on his $6 million loan, the company was immediately calling in the entire loan and had filed suit in federal court. No thirty-day grace period, nothing. What bastards!

That was ten, going on eleven years ago. Edwig Messinger still believed in Puerto Rico's potential role in creating an interdependence of nations of the American (Western) Hemisphere. It would be the first step in developing that noble concept through Las Brisas del Caribe, the project he had planned for the 750 acres he had owned on the rolling hills overlooking the ever-blue Caribbean on the east coast of the island. The project would have acted—how had he put it? He pulled the sheet of paper out of the back of the notebook he carried at all times in his black shoulder bag that converted into a brief case for business meetings. Not that many recently, he acknowledged, but not too sadly because he knew that things would pick up again once he found the proper investors with intelligence and insight. He reread: "The project will act as a catalytic force in a historic movement that, for the first time since the Golden Age of Ancient Greece, will propel mankind to attain its human potential."

He would have set up on the property, the Golden Age Institute. Within the Institute would have been a World Study Center for Creative Leisure, which would have explored beneficial changes in human behavior. A revolution in values. The end of human greed. All of us would be put on the road toward human fulfillment. A new world system. A humanistic future. Heavy stuff. But he still believed.

Along with some New York investors, he had bought the property for a song from a bankrupt Spanish developer. Those were the days, when he had gotten into real estate. The island was wide open then for all kinds of business deals. *Everyone* was buying, selling, wheeling, dealing.

Now he just about survived pedaling timeshares, apartments and homes for a local company. The irony, of course was that he couldn't find a place he could now call his own home.

His house in Old San Juan with the fifteen-foot-high

waterfall flowing down the far wall beneath the wood-beamed ceiling and into a little pond, white lilies floating on top. The pond separated from the indoor pool by a polished stone walkway. The pool emptied, then carpeted when events are held. Carpeted ramps lead in and out of the pool area. Ceiling fans whirring overhead along with the air-conditioning for the big crowds that gather. Red and blue striped umbrellas cover tables in the back patio. Paintings, prints by local artists cover the walls. Local strolling musicians. The guitar player owns the bodega down the street, two of his sons scrape guiros. He hires friends, neighbors. They sing, "En Mi Viejo San Juan."

The Glory Days, when Edwig Messinger was moving up, up and on his way. Those days *will* return.

Messinger downed the rest of his beer. His lanky body was tired from the day's running around and he still felt tense. A pain was still embedded in his high forehead. He ordered a Courvoisier. A few people came in and out of the bar area, downed a drink or two, left. Itwas after eleven and Edwig now was the only customer there. He drank his Courvoisier, ordered another.

The bad, early days in Wilmington. His old man, the junk dealer. Stupid German immigrant. Continually boxing his son around the head for reading books, not helping the old man pick up the city's debris. Mother dies two days after his tenth birthday. At sixteen, he, Edwig, runs far, far away to

Chicago, then Miami, then San Juan, Puerto Rico.

The better days. Living in one room at the Colonial Guesthouse, befriending Charlie Jones, an old swimming instructor who teaches him scuba diving. He becomes adept, gets a job at the Caribe Hilton, where he meets Phyllis. Incredibly, she also is from Wilmington. They both graduated from Concord High, he four years earlier. He runs the scuba diving concession at the hotel and gives her diving lessons. Convinces her to stay an extra week (he gets her a great discount), then another week (he pays), then asks her to move in with him. She goes back to Wilmington, quits her job as a hotel clerk in the DuPont building, and returns. Two months living together, then they marry.

Early years of carefree living. Not rich, but not poor because he gets lots of freebies at the hotel, and the other places where he runs his scuba diving concessions. Then the kids, Sheila, then Stanley, then branching out into real estate, then the Fajardo purchase, a beautiful piece of real estate about a 90-minute drive from San Juan. At first he wants to develop the land into nothing more than homes for the wealthy movers and shakers from the states who want a second home on the island. He sells the idea right away, gets the loan to start building. Then, after greasing palms, making political contributions for the proper permits, along comes Hurricane Alma. It knocks to pieces the few houses he started building. *And then, The Great Awakening. The understanding of the way of the world, which certainly needs changing from grubby greedy to honorably humanistic.*

He will construct in La Brisas del Caribe the first of what will be humanistic villages on the island, then he will build them all over the Caribbean. He will pattern these villages on the "polis" of Ancient Greece. He reads and reads and reads and he finds that Kitto quoted Pericles as saying the polis is not just a place to inhabit, but that it should encompass an entire way of life that develops both the mind and the character of its citizens. It all dovetails with the growing concept of leisure living. The inhabitants of the polis will be able to develop their lives within a leisure living atmosphere, but with a different definition of that living style than what has been generally accepted: passing time in meaningless passive pursuits or buying, buying. The new definition, the new living experience, will revolve around creative activities that will assure the participants that they are involved in being something.

To...be...something. What a fantastic concept! Where the greatness of the past will meet the potential of the future. Human potential, fulfillment, enrichment, self- esteem, self-actualization!

He plans the first Puerto Rico polis to encompass the whole communal life of its 5,040 inhabitants (Plato's exact number for the ideal polis).

The Glory Days. Buying his Old San Juan home, using it for seminars, lectures led by those at the top of their field: scientists, educators, psychologists, sociologists, anthropologists, environmentalists, futurists, planners, artists, musicians, sports figures, entertainers—all devoted to a life of creative leisure. Al Toffler, Bucky Fuller, Jim Rouse, Ivan Illich, Paulo Friere, John Cage, Marshall McLuhan. Yes, much of the budget goes to hosting these seers at the luxury hotels around San Juan, but it's more than worth it, spending the money for the incredible, invaluable insights they share. He puts local talent, college professors, artists (even some con artists) on the payroll. He calls press conferences. In truth, he loves the attention. He understands that he has the humbleness of the true egocentric. Poor kid from Wilmington, junk dealing, ignorant, son-beating father. All that behind him now.

He enters into talks with officials of the Puerto Rico government and even with federal officials in Washington to try to get them to help underwrite the $100 million-plus project. They all appear interested, fascinated—he believes he is on the verge of getting additional funds. Then...they call in his loan! He fights them in court.

The sad days. The horrible days. He goes into deep debt hiring lawyers. Phyllis takes the kids, returns to Wilmington.

She can't put up with it anymore. All he talks about is the project, how it (he) will save the world. She says he's going crazy and driving her and the kids nuts too. He lives with Plato, his German Shepherd. Plato breaks from his leash, is run over on the Boulevard del Valle. Comes home squealing, crying, dying.

He no longer makes mortgage payments. After a fruitless day at the Industrial Development Company, making still another "last-ditch" effort to have the government adopt the project, take it over, finance it—he wil merely be an advisor. On his return "home," he is greeted by a crowd of scavengers going through his furniture, furnishings, artworks, clothes, everything once inside now piled up like trash on the sidewalk. His large eyes popping (they often did). He prepares to battle his way through to the front door. Then he decides he will leave everything to the scavengers, never set foot in that house again.

"One more Courvoisier, please."

"Sure thing," said Perry the bartender.

A tired-looking, sort of floozy looking, middle-aged blonde took a seat at the bar two stools from Edwig. She bent over the bar to pat Perry's arm as he washed out glasses.

"A scotch-and-soda, please," she said. "Make it a Chivas."

"Right," said Perry.

"How's it going?" she asked the bartender.

"It's going," said Perry. "You okay?"

"You don't want to hear," she said, then turned to Edwig and winked. "He's everybody's sounding board. And, boy, there are characters galore around here." Edwig smiled, gave an agreeable nod.

"Well, another day and I'll be back home," Sally announced. "It'll be a relief. I got myself into something pretty weird here. Some vacation." She closed her eyes and slowly shook her head. "I mean I'm taking care of this guy who tried to, who sure as hell robbed me, the sonovabitch. Well, he ain't a complete sonovabitch. He's…what? A sad case. A single parent. A screwed up guy. Like he's the first one I ever met. Right!

"Look, here's the thing, this guy, this Hector-Jesus, he keeps apologizing to me, he swears to me he's gonna get a regular job, he asked me to just take care of his son, Jesus Junior, who he keeps saying he would die for—the kid's not even two years old—would I take care of him till he, Jesus Senior, gets back on his feet? He, the father, had this asthma attack, which is giving him breathing problems and put him out of commission for days. So I been going over there at nights, after I'm working days helping out a friend of my husband Joe, the man's secretary took an emergency vacation. Then I been cooking dinner for them, Jesus one and

Jesus two, and helping clean up the kid and the house. That kid, with eyes so big and brown and looking into your heart, it pains."

Sally took a large gulp of her drink. "I don't know why I'm spending my vacation doing this stuff, but anyway tomorrow night is the last night and I'll be going home to Joe, where I should be, taking care of him. So I arranged with Carmencita to go to el jerko's house after she finished work at the guesthouse here to make sure the kid's eating and is all right. A hundred bucks for the week, but it's worth it. The jerk should be on his feet by then. He'd better be!"

Perry washed out glasses. Edwig snuck a glance at Sally, who was now looking deep into her glass. Was she expecting some message to pop up, thanking her for being such a good person?

Don't you be a jerk too, Edwig told himself. He would take a chance.

"Sounds like you're having a weird vacation, if you could call it that." He tried to give her a very sympathetic smile, feeling stupid for repeating her earlier sentiment.

Sally looked over to Edwig, as though just realizing he was seated a couple of stools from her. "Yeah, weird," she said.

"Have you had a chance to visit Old San Juan or get out on the island?"

"The first week I was here it rained practically every day. I spent the time getting robbed by the one-armed bandits in the casino there, before I met the one with two arms. I ain't had a chance to really relax on the beach. I'm going home from a 'vacation' in Puerto Rico without a suntan," Sally said, as though few things could be more ridiculous.

"Have you been to El Yunque?"

"What's that?"

"El Yunque, the rain forest."

"I didn't come down here for no rain. I *thought* I was coming for the sun."

Edwig smiled. He liked a woman with a sense of humor. Actually, he was feeling good for the first time in days, maybe even weeks. The woman seemed to be sympathetic. She deserved to have had a more enjoyable vacation.

"May I introduce myself? May I also buy you a drink?"

"I'm Sally," she said, beating him to the introduction. "And you can buy me all the drinks you want."

Edwig's left eye twitched. He sensed...something. "Ed," he said. "Ed Messinger."

"So Ed, what do you do around here?" Sally asked.

"Here?"

"Yeah, here, in Puerto Rico. Do you live here or are you a tourist?"

"I'm a resident of the island. Have been for the past

fifteen years."

"Really? Wow! You must really like living here."

Edwig nodded, smiled. "I suppose you could say that."

"Could *you* say that? I mean, fifteen years on an island."

Edwig signaled Perry to replace their drinks with new ones. Could he say that? Well, he certainly could have during The Glory Days.

"Let me put it this way: Puerto Rico was and still could be a wonderful place to live. The beaches, the rolling mountains, the wonderful Old City. The people, most of them, are so…kind, *simpático*. They deserve better. And the potential is here for the island to become a prime catalyst for the improvement of mankind."

He drank his cognac. Sally screwed up her face. What the hell was he talking about?

Edwig sensed the question on her face. "A dream," he said. "A dream that was very close to becoming a wonderful reality."

Sally took a deep breath, yet she smiled at Edwig. "Yeah, *right!*"

Was she thinking, 'one more character?' He'd show her that he was for real, a legitimate person with a very possible future success and prominence.

"Listen," he said. "I have an idea. I know you are going home soon, but would you have one more day, so that I could show you the physical and even the idealistic beauty of the island?"

Sally rubbed her mouth, then placed her index fingers at the corners of her eyes and rubbed the little hard edges. "My plane leaves tomorrow at seven fifteen in the evening."

"I'll bring you back by then. In fact you can take your luggage with you and I'll drive you right out to the airport."

Sally looked at Edwig, squinted and frowned. Then she shrugged. "I'm going to bed now," she said. "I'll meet you here at nine in the morning and you can show me around, wherever the hell you want to show me." She finished the rest of her drink, blew Perry a kiss, nodded to Edwig, lowered herself off the bar stool and walked straight up to her room across from the front desk.

She was deep in a dream of searching with mounting frustration and sadness for her missing Madonna medallion when a sharp rap on the door awoke her.

"What? What?"

"It's me, Ed from last night."

"Ed who?"

"Ed Messinger. We met last night at the bar. I'm going to take you for a little trip before you go home this evening, remember?"

Aw, damn, Sally had hoped the guy wouldn't show up. As soon as she got into bed last night, she realized what she really wanted to do on her last day was to relax on the beach.

This has been one hell of a vacation. Maybe she should start doing what she wanted for a change, tell this guy she was feeling sick, couldn't make the trip. Instead, she was giving into the wishes of every needy jerk she was meeting here.

"Give me fifteen minutes," she said through the door.

Sally got dressed in white slacks and a sleeveless black blouse, and put her hair, still damp from the shower, in a ponytail. Black mascara under her large brown eyes, bright red lips, some wrinkles showing through, despite the makeup. Still, not bad-looking.

She came out to the patio. "I need some coffee," she said.

Edwig looked at his watch. Almost ten o'clock. "Is it okay, if we get it to go?"

"Fine," said Sally, somewhat sourly.

"Could we get a container of coffee to go?" Edwig asked Bernardo, who was in the small kitchen behind the bar.

"No problem."

Sally started sipping the coffee as they got outside and crossed the street to get to Edwig's Lincoln Continental, which looked more than a little worse for wear. The roof was peeling and there were some bends in the fenders.

Sally got in the passenger's seat and Edwig pulled the car

out.

"So, where we going?"

"Do you have your bathing suit?" Edwig looked at the big straw bag between Sally's legs.

"I sure do."

"Good, our first stop will be Luquillo Beach. Then we'll go on to El Yunque, the rain forest. Then…well, I want you to see something very interesting, something very close to me."

"Oh, really?" Sally gave Edwig a sideways glance. "I hope it ain't *that* close."

"No…yes. Well, you'll see."

Sally closed her eyes and nodded. "Whatever. Let's get the show on the road."

It took about an hour and a half to get to the beach at Luquillo. Tall palm trees gave finger waves all over the place. Real white sand. Real blue water. And not crowded at all. It beat the hell out of Coney, even Jones Beach, thought Sally.

Sally put on her blue one-piece in a changing room and ran laughing into the water. Edwig dove in after her. He was swimming and diving like crazy with tubes and masks and scuba tanks he got from the trunk of his car and even taught her how to snorkel with a mask and a tube and rubber fins. They had a couple of wonderful hours there, then ate at one of the food kiosks along the road. Sally insisted on paying after they feasted on codfish fritters. "They're called, *bacalaitos,"* Edwig instructed and they washed them down and they washed them down with piña coladas.

They took off for the rain forest, a half-hour drive along narrow, bumpy, curvy roads. They parked at the visitor's center, hiked along dense forest trails, smelled things blooming and decaying, saw pink and white orchids growing on branches—some no larger than the top joint of Sally's pinky—rested by a beautiful waterfall. They went back for the car, drove to the very top of a mountain, climbed up the tower there. So far, no rain, but clouds were creeping up the sides of the mountain.

"This tower," Edwig intoned, like he was talking to a group of tourists, "is named after the ancient Taino god, Yúcahu, said to have lived here on the mountain top. He was the god of fertility."

"With kids all over the place on the island, he didn't do a bad job," Sally said.

"Okay," Ed said. "Now, I want you to see something really special."

Another thirty to forty minutes on often rutted roads with shacks along the sides, climbing up and swerving down hillsides and across valleys, then way up to a sweeping view of other green-clotted hills and valleys, and way down there a strip of white sand and the sea.

"There it is," said Edwig proudly, as if he had

something to do with producing the scenery below. "That's Las Brisas del Caribe. Seven hundred and fifty acres of magnificent rolling hills and verdant valleys and one-half a mile of pristine beach. It takes your breath away, right?"

He looked at Sally, as though he expected to see her gasping.

"Real pretty," she said.

"Breathtakingly beautiful. And I owned it all—until those bastards took it away from me!"

There were actually tears in his eyes. What the hell was he talking about? "What bastards? Who took what?"

Edwig's face screwed up, then his eyes popped. "You don't know about this, right?" He seemed angry, like Sally was denying something she should have known about. This was getting weird. Then his face relaxed. "Of course, of course. You don't live here. It was all over the papers and on the TV here. It was mentioned in the book, *The Coming Way of the World* by Harvey Kleinman, the well-known environmental-leisure living futurist. Let's see, I think I have a copy of..."

He turned to the back seat and picked up his black leather zip-around bag briefcase. He took out many sheets of paper, shuffled through them, found what he was looking for. "I copied a couple of pages from Kleinman's book. Okay, here's a couple of graphs." He read:

"A bright, young real estate investor, Edwig Messinger, was able to buy up several hundred acres of magnificent rolling hills, verdant valleys and half a mile of pristine beach on the east coast of the U. S. Commonwealth of Puerto Rico, located in the Lesser Antilles of the Caribbean. The forward-looking Delaware native, who first planned a conventional resort area for tourists and purchasers of second-homes, had a change of heart after learning about the leisure living movement.

"Messinger understood the importance of the integration into his project of the collected transdisciplinary research on active living. Opportunities for leisure studies/recreation on active living include studies of environmental, life span and motivational influences; greater use of objective measures of physical activity; and forming partnerships with allied industries to study physical activity. Among suggestions for facilitating such studies are training seminars for leisure recreation researchers in active living research methods, changes in point allocation on grant proposals, providing incentives for transdisciplinary collaboration, and special research issues. Among other things..."

"Yeah, okay," Sally said. "I get the idea." Whatever it was, it sounded like a load of bullshit.

"So I had the loans to start the development and I was going to start building real soon, after collating the incredible input from the experts who lent their time to this plan and... *what the hell is that?!"*

"What?" Sally jumped in her car seat along with Edwig.

"That! That! Over there." Edwig was pointing to something outside the side window. He quickly got out of the car. Sally got out on the other side.

"C'mere," Edwig told Sally. "Look at that."

She went around the front of the car to look down the hillside where Edwig was pointing. What she saw were about five or six plywood, corrugated tin-roofed shacks cluttered together, not far from the beach. They looked like so many of the shacks they had passed along the road.

"So?" Sally wondered how nutty this guy actually was.

"Those houses down there. They're squatters. They've taken over the land. Okay, the economy is close to tanking and the friggin' bank can't get rid of the land, which is why I still have a chance. I've got some crucial meetings with possible investors in the next couple of weeks. But now with these squatters—you know how hard it is to get them off the land? People have been killed, both squatters and police. The value of the land plummets." Edwig gave the fender of his Lincoln Continental a sharp slap. "But if you leave them living down there, soon you have a community of hundreds. Then the stories come out in the papers, on TV. Then the bank finds out and the government gets involved, the bulldozers, the screaming women, the crying kids, the men get their machetes, the police, fights, shots, the National Guard. *Damn!*"

Sally grunted.

Edwig's face had turned red. Now it was going pale and hard and resolute. His lips pursed and he nodded, as though daring anyone to disagree. "I'm going down there to speak to those people, so that they understand how disastrous it could be for them, for the future—for *all* of us."

Oh, for Christsake! "What time is it?" Sally asked. She had left her watch in her straw bag when she changed to go swimming.

"It's time," Edwig answered, "for all of us to consider the consequences of our actions."

Edgardo weaved down the hillside through lush green shrubs and brambles and Sally, following but not knowing why the hell she was, got her sandaled feet all cut up. *Sonovabitch!*

They reached a cleared area where the five shacks stood practically on top of one another. Two dogs came up to bark at and smell the feet of the newcomers, roosters crowed somewhere behind the houses.

Edwig went up to the first house they approached and knocked on the door. A very old lady peeked out of a window next to the door.

Edwig tried a winning smile. *"Hola, abuelita,"* he said.

The wrinkled, toothless, grandmotherly woman returned a shaky smile. "No home," she said. "No home." She closed the paneled window from inside.

"What are we doing here?" Sally asked, only half-expecting a reasonable answer.

Before Edwig could answer, the front door opened. A young, heavy-set woman with light green eyes and holding a baby to her breast smiled shyly. "Please excuse grandma," the woman said. "Can I help you?"

"She speaks English like an American," Sally said.

"That's because I was born and raised in the Bronx," the young woman said with a smile.

"That's swell," said Sally.

Edwig said: "Is your husband home by any chance?"

"He's out in the community garden over there," the young woman said, waving to some place behind the five shacks. "We're growing vegetables," she said with a wide smile. "By the way, my name is Juanita."

Sally introduced herself and Edwig.

"I'll get my husband," Juanita said, coming out with the baby at her breast.

Sally put out her hands. "I'll hold…"

"It's okay," said Juanita. "You see I have him in this little harness I made from some cloth and buttons, so I can walk with him. He's secure and happy in there." She went along the dirt path in front of the houses and disappeared behind the last one.

"So what the hell are we here for?" asked Sally.

"I want to meet the man of the house," Edwig responded.

"Why?"

"We have some things to discuss."

Jes-us Christ! "Hey, it's getting late. We got to start back soon. I haven't officially checked out yet and I got some more things to do before I get to the airport."

"Don't worry. This is important," Edwig said.

The husband appeared, a short, muscular guy with a bushy mustache, wearing a sleeveless undershirt and an unraveling straw farmer's hat. Running in front of him and giggling, were a boy and a girl of seven or eight. Juanita and the baby brought up the rear.

Wiping his hand on the side of his jeans, the guy introduced himself. "José Ramírez. A sus *ordenes."* He nodded to Sally and said to Edwig:*"¿Que tal, amigo?* You need somesin'?"

"I was just wondering," Edwig said. "How long you and your…neighbors have been living on this land?"

José's eyes narrowed. "Why you ask? You from the government?"

"No, no," Edwig assured José, whose face relaxed.

"You and your woman wanna move here?" he said with a wide grin.

"No, we, I…I want to help you before people try to move you off the land."

"Nobody going to move us nowhere," José said, his eyes narrowing. Then he smiled widely again. "We been here about a month, after the factory over there"—he nodded up to the top of the hill—"when it shut down and I was no more the janitor, we couldn't pay the rent in the other place"—he nodded up the hill again—"and Juanita and me we build the house for us and the kids and my mom, so we livin' here now. How you gonna help?"

"Well, it's just that…"

Let's get the hell out of here, thought Sally.

"You want some coffee?" Juanita said. "Please, come into our home."

"That would be wonderful," Edwig said.

"Hey, it's getting late," Sally told Edwig.

"We can't say no," Edwig whispered. "It would be impolite."

Sally rolled her eyes. If she missed that goddamn flight…

"Just a few minutes," Edwig said. "Besides I've got to tell them."

They entered the shack. There was one large room and two back areas separated by hanging curtains. In the back of the room was a large, old refrigerator, an ancient looking four-burner stove, one long rectangular table, five straw-backed chairs and a couple of cabinets. Off to the side were two straw-backed rockers—the grandma sitting on one of them, mumbling to herself—as well as a crib and a playpen. On the other side, a hammock hung from the ceiling beams. The wood-paneled floor was swept clean. Sally didn't ask where the dishes and clothes were washed, where the latrine and shower were, how the three adults, two children and one baby managed to live in here.

Juanita, who put the sleeping baby in the crib while the two other kids disappeared giggling behind one of the curtains, saw Sally and Edwig looking around with open mouths.

"Little by little," she said. She went to the long table and pulled a cord hanging from a bare bulb, which lit up. "Already, electricity," she said. "José and our neighbors, they know how to get the electricity. Soon we will have running water. It's not that bad," Juanita said. "We've got hens in the back that give us eggs and there's mango and lemon trees and the beach is right below. We got a boat down there and we catch fish."

Juanita went to the ancient stove and switched on a gas burner and a pot of coffee perked. Juanita served Sally, Edwig and her husband mugs of coffee and gave one to grandma silently rocking in her chair. She put a plate of crackers on the table, a bottle of Cheez Whiz, a knife for spreading and paper napkins. "Please help yourselves," she said. José spread the cheesy stuff on four crackers and handed them around.

"Muchas gracias," said Edwig. Then, looking down at his cracker, he said, "But the land, it isn't yours."

"We hear it belong to the government," said José. "They see we here, they have to let us live here because there ain't no place else we can go."

"Usufruct," said Juanita.

"Juanita know the big words," José said. "She was a teacher before we got the kids."

"Only a substitute," Juanita said. "I still have a year to go for a teaching degree." Then she said: "Under usufruct, we can use the land if we return it in the same condition. When José gets another job and we get enough money together so I can get my teaching certificate and we move into a real home, we will destroy this house and make everything like it was."

"No, no," said Edwig. "Under the usufruct law here, the land must belong to the government. But this land you are living on cannot be issued as usufruct because it does *not* belong to the government. You see…"

For Christsake! thought Sally. What the hell were they talking about?

"You see," Edwig said. "The land you are living on

belongs to the bank."

"The bank?" José looked at his wife. She shrugged.

"The bank got it. They took it away—from me. I used to own this land. And I plan to get it back. To build a project that will resolve the problems of Puerto Rico, and perhaps the world. Itwill bring humanity back into the way we should treat one another. Things will work differently. People, like you and us, we will be put first, not the banks and other unbridled capitalist and governmental entities."

José and Juanita exchanged confused looks. Then they looked at Sally. Sally shrugged apologetically.

Edwig continued in a most reasonable tone: "So you see, you and your neighbors must leave now, before the word is out and the bulldozers come to save this valuable land for the bank, which is trying, and will certainly one day succeed, in selling it. But I believe that I can convince new investors to put up the money needed for me to reclaim the land and tum the property into a meaningful way of life for its inhabitants, and that the success will spur others to adopt the method of true living that begins here."

Sally got up. "Let's go. I got a plane to make. We gotta go— now!"

Edwig offered a sheepish smile all around, looking as though, Sally thought, he realized the listeners may not have been ready to learn the "truth" of their situation and, for that matter, of the whole goddamn future.

As they were leaving, Sally whispered to Juanita: "Sorry."

Juanita shrugged. "Not to worry," she said with a half-smile. "We *all* got problems."

Sally turned and opened her purse. She thumbed off five from the roll of twenties from her work for Teamster Pete, then went back to the table, picked up a leftover cracker and put it in her mouth, as though hunger made her return there. She slipped the bills under a coffee mug.

On the practically conversation-less trip back to San Juan, the new plan developed. La Brisas del Caribe would still be the first Golden Age settlement, but it would now be for the landless poor!

Edwig would go to the media, to the government, both in San Juan and Washington, to present his plan. The local government, with federal aid, would purchase the land from the bank. He would take charge of the project, appeal to the local business community for help. He saw a series of telethons, the entire community getting behind this incredible idealistic experiment. His release to the media would read: "The landless poor will be given homes and taught marketable skills while deriving the benefits of living in a future creative environment that harkens back to the greatest age of the Ancient World."

Not only would he bring back all the experts from the worlds of science, the arts and other intellectual disciples, he would also arrange for carpenters, plumbers, electricians, masons, practical nurses, auto mechanics, chefs to offer input into the job training programs that would be an integral part in the new Las Brisas.

The training programs, as well as the lectures, would be offered as much as possible under the shade of the mango and the lemon trees, in a setting not unlike Plato's Academy. He could pull it off. He knew he could. And he wanted this Sally, who had related well to these poor people, to stay here in Puerto Rico to help.

He would appeal to the goodness he had seen inside her. He was sure she would agree to stay on and help make a wonderful reality of the first step toward a truly humanistic future.

Chapter 11

That's it! She's moved her last goddamn paper. Now he couldn't find the damn thing!

Burt Cherry had fallen asleep while writing his appeal of the decision to deny his motion for reconsideration. He was writing it out longhand on one of the myriad of yellow ruled pads piled around the room. When he awoke the pad was at the foot of the bed. When he left the room to go up the street to Kasalta bakery for a late breakfast *(mallorca tostada, relleno de papas* and two cups of coffee), the pad was still at the foot of the bed. When he returned to his room, ready to finish the appeal, the bed was made, his pads, papers, folders, portfolios, clipped articles, newspapers, magazines, photos of GM vehicles dating way back and assorted single sheets and scraps of paper were all neatly stacked around the room, the yellow ruled pads mixed in with all the rest.

Where the hell was the pad he had written on last night? He went through the piles, did not find the pad. He went through the piles again; again didn't find it. Again, and again and again. Then, finally, there it was, between the first two pages of the Feb. 5, 1967 edition of *the New York Times* with the front page headline: "Detective in Nader Case Says General Motors Altered Papers."

He was getting lightheaded, but not dizzy enough not to do what had to be done. He had to get the hell out of now! Get a room where no one would be messing with his papers. In the Old City, as close as possible to the federal courthouse, so he could check every goddamn day how the motions and the writs and the appeals were going, bugging the court clerks, so they'll complain to the judges' clerks, so they'll take it up with their dishonorable honors who will finally take deep, long looks at what he has been saying for decades in his documents about the scandalous underhanded machinations of General Motors. And they'll finally understand that Mr. Burt Cherry is a true seeker of justice, which will bite into what is left of their shrunken consciences. And to save that minute part of the ideals they once possessed (possibly), the once jeering now apologetic judges will rule in favor of what is fair and just and against the grotesque greed which is General Motors. So pack up, which in between a sneezing fit, he did. With shipping tape, he restructured the many flattened-out cartons stored in the room's closet from his last move.

The few clothes he had fit into two cartons and his documents were piled into the other boxes. The boxes were piled onto the dolly he also had stored away. He zipped up his wonderful Olivetti Lettera 22 in its light blue carrying case with the black strip down the middle and put it on top of the boxes. He wheeled the dolly from his first floor room at the back of the guesthouse to the front desk. No one was there for a change.

He parked the dolly and went looking for Bernardo. Bernardo was on the second floor hammering a screen into a window.

"I'm moving out," Burt said. "How much do I owe you?"

Bernardo stopped hammering. "Is something wrong, Mr. Cherry?"

"Not any more wrong than usual," Bert said.

Bernardo frowned, gave a questioning nod.

"Never mind. It ain't something that's gonna be changed. But it's time for me to change where I'm living. I gotta be closer to what is my main interest right now."

"Is there anything…?"

"No, no, that's okay. You're a good guy. Just tell me what I owe you."

"Let's go down to the office. I think you are just a week behind on your rent."

They went downstairs. Burt paid the week's back rent and was left with zilch in his wallet. He had to go to the bank. He had to get a job.

He rolled his dolly out the door, clunking it down the front steps, making sure with one hand that the typewriter wouldn't topple over. His goddamn nose was dripping again!

He put the dolly against the balcony ledge, got the hanky out his back pocket and blew his nose. He would wash out the hanky as soon as he got to his new place. He grabbed the dolly handles and steered his stuff along the street heading for McLeary, which would lead him onto Ashford, named after the Americano doctor who helped the PRs get rid of hookworm, then over the Dos Hermanos Bridge, named after the two brothers who brought telephone service to the island, then around past the Normandie Hotel that was built to resemble the liner of the same name by some nutty millionaire to impress some broad, then by the stadium where major leaguers used to play in the winter until Bithorn stadium was built out in Hato Rey, onto the ocean road leading into Old San Juan, founded in the year 1521. Burt made sure to know all this shuff when he first came down to the island. You can't be *completely* ignorant of your surroundings.

After a couple of hours, with his short-sleeved shirt sticking to his back, his legs and arms shaking with both numbness and pain, his fingers feeling paralyzed; how the hell he made it to Old San Juan without collapsing, he'd never know.

He went to the Banco Popular up from the waterfront, parking his dolly inside where he could keep an eye on it. He filled out a withdrawal slip for a hundred dollars.

"Sorry, sir," said the bank clerk, a young guy with a mosquito mustache, "but only have you twenty-five dollars in your account."

Goddamn it!

"Gimme the twenty-five,"

Cousin Willy: his only hope. He'll call, reverse the charges. Two years ago, he'd lent him $1,000 to help start up the toy store. It was doing okay until the goddamn big-box stores moved in. Still, he should be able to pay back a couple of hundred. Ask Willy to wire the money, get a cheap room in the Old City before he gets settled in again. Go to the hotels, get a job washing dishes. He'd done it before. He was an ace pot-and-pan man.

He rolled the dolly across to the small, tree-shaded plaza that was just a stone's throw from the post office-federal courthouse. Traffic rumbled past, wild parrots cheeped in the trees, life's hangers-on sat on the benches talking to each other or themselves. He sat for a couple of minutes, then rolled the dolly to the public phones in front of the courthouse.

Willy didn't answer. He tried a couple more times. Not even a goddamn answering machine.

He rolled the dolly back to the plazoleta. He went through the top box below his typewriter and pulled out the yellow lined pad with his latest, half-written appeal. He worked on the appeal for a couple of hours.

It was finished. A thing of beauty.

Dusk was coming on. The courts and the clerk's office, were of course, closed for the day. He brought the dolly across to the phones again. No answer. He'd try tomorrow. At least he had enough for bread and coffee. No need to eat now. Tomorrow morning.

He settled back on the park bench, his dolly at the side of the bench. It could be a long, night. Tough. He was just across the street from the courthouse. Who—especially if the "who" was he—could ask for anything more?

Chapter 12

It surely wasn't like the old days, when he would introduce Al Toffler or Bucky Fuller or Jim Rouse or Ivan Illich, then sit back as they took over, presenting their incredible ideas and with great seriousness and good humor, answer the questions from the press. Now he was on his own. He had convinced Bernardo, the owner of the guesthouse where he now lived, to turn over the patio to him for the early morning press conference. He would pay for the coffee and sweet rolls offered to the reporters, photographers, cameramen, et al.

Edwig had moved the tables to the back of the patio and set out the chairs in rows. He kept one table up front and sat behind the documents piled on top of it. So far, there were exactly two reporters—one from *Claridad,* which supported independence for the island, and a radio reporter who would tape his remarks and undoubtedly cut them to pieces for later broadcast—and a freelance female photographer from no media in particular. Some old guy he didn't recognize sat on a chair in one of the back rows. It was fifteen minutes past the announced starting time for the conference.

Ten years ago, the place would have been packed with TV lights, snaking cables, mikes up on the table for live broadcasts, flashing cameras. Where the hell was everybody?

The fickle press. It no longer saw him and his project as "newsworthy," even though his new efforts would take a giant step toward alleviating poverty. Well, in truth, the press, one more member of the local establishment, would be the last to know what was truly newsworthy.

"There is coffee and snacks at the table by the bar," Edwig told those who had shown up. "Let's just wait a few more…"

"Hey, screw the coffee and cake," said the radio reporter. "I got three more press conferences to cover before noon."

"All right, all right," Edwig said. "We'll begin and when the others show up, recapitulate."

"Yeah, great," said the radio guy, who looked like the middle-aged hack he was, who got all those non-exclusive "exclusives" that polluted the local airwaves.

Edwig picked up some sheets of paper, looked down, then looked up and said: "Okay, allow me to begin this news conference." He went to his prepared statement. "I will begin by announcing that on a recent visit in the glorious hills around the East Coast town of Fajardo, to a poor, hard-working family of 'squatters. ' I use the quotation marks around the word because of its derogatory connotation, which did not fit this and I'm sure other families, in similar situations. Well, during the visit to these 'squatters,' I had a revelation. For perhaps the first time, I understood how to go about easing the plight of the poor, here in Puerto Rico, and, by extension, because of its remarkably available applicability, to other islands, countries, nations. All that is needed is the *will*. Where there is a *will,* there is an end to poverty throughout the world."

Edwig went on to detail his project, how he would present his plan to officials both in San Juan and Washington, how the local government would get federal aid to purchase the land from the bank, how he would appeal to the business community for help, how homes would be built and given to the landless poor, who would be trained for jobs.

After several minutes of Edwig's spiel, the radio-reporter said in a stage whisper, *"Que mierda.* What a bunch of bullshit." The young guy from the hard-left weekly said nothing. While he took notes, he kept shaking his head and breaking into grimacing grins. The photographer snapped a few photos of Edwig speaking, the back of the heads of the two reporters amid the rows of empty chairs, then left.

"All right," said Edwig, "I'm ready to take questions."

Packing up his equipment, the radio reporter again stage-whispered: "That was a friggin' waste of time." But the young reporter from *Claridad* did have a question, and a statement, and another question. And another statement.

"May I ask you, sir, what makes you think that both the colonial government of Puerto Rico and their masters in Washington have any interest in putting an end to poverty here or anywhere on earth? I'm sure you realize the capitalist system only thrives *because* of the prevalence of poverty in the world. Capitalism, sir, is an economic system that depends on poverty and reproduces it."

"Well, yes and no," said Edwig.

"How would you answer, sir, the charges that are sure to be made, that your plan is nothing more than more ideological weaponry for imperialism, since the plan fosters the illusion that capitalism can be transformed into a caring and compassionate system? I'm sure you're aware, sir, that capitalism produces poverty and cannot possibly alleviate it without negating itself as a system of production. Poverty exists because the economic system is organized in ways that encourage the accumulation of wealth at one end and abject poverty on the other end."

"I wouldn't say that," said Edwig.

"Well, then, what *would* you say?"

"Look, we have to work within the system we live in or…"

"Yes?" The young guy put a factitious smile on his smooth, barely shave-worthy face.

"Well, you want to change the system, you have to start a revolution."

"Yes?"

"Come on! People die in revolutions. Those things never work out."

The skin around the young reporter's eyes creased in mock pain. "How terrible!" he said. "You think that? That is what you believe?"

Edwig took a deep breath. "Look, we're talking poverty here, not revolution. The question is, how do we eliminate poverty within the system that we have? Should Puerto Rico become a state? Should it have more autonomy under commonwealth? Or should Washington make it an independent nation? Which would be the best way to do away with the island's poverty?"

"Do you truly know poverty?" the reporter-antagonist asked.

"Well, I…. Hey, what do *you* know about poverty?"

"The only thing I know," said the young reporter, whom Edwig was sure was barely out of college, "is that if I had to live in the circumstances of those you call 'squatters,' and we call 'land retrievers,' and I knew that the only way out of my situation was through revolution, I would actually favor it."

Edwig's eyebrows shot up. "I really wonder how many of the poor on the island would agree with you."

"Do you know the answer to that? Have you had that experience that the poor of the island have had, and therefore can answer for them?"

"Well, look…"

"Yes?"

"Well…okay, thanks for coming."

The reporter left and Edwig started putting the table and chairs back as they were.

Damnit! What, indeed does he, Edwig Messinger, know about real poverty? Not too damn much. So what will he do about it? Continue to present his project. It certainly makes more sense than a Cuba-style revolution here.

But look at today's measly turnout. Like everything else that filters down from the States, so have the Reagan years. No one cares about the poor any more.

Well, let's be honest, Edwig. People remember that your last project literally never got off the ground,

Why couldn't he present a cogent argument to that just-weaned reporter? Well, because… . Well, now he knows what he has to do. Now he knows—for sure.

He has few, if any, commitments, let alone close contacts, especially since Sally went back to the states. She had humored him that she might stay, or come back to work on the project, then she was off. No goodbye. Nothing.

So he would go out there again, ask for help in building a house, a shack, anything over his head. Pay them? No, that wouldn't be right. He'd be living like them. After—months, years?—of having lived the life of a squatter, he would present his plan again. Yes! He would live poverty and after his experiences, people would be forced to listen and, most important, to act! They would understand and accept that the time had come for the project, the Golden Age for the Landless Poor.

As he was about to return to his room, the old guy who sat through the press conference moved toward him. He introduced himself as Francisco Guerrero. "I'm called Cisco and I have lived seemingly forever in a room on the second floor. I just want to tell you, sir, that I enjoyed your presentation. Your heart is, indeed, in the right place. I wish you luck. You have a noble idea."

"Thank you," said Edwig.

They shook hands.

Noble, Edwig said to himself as he headed back to his room. This old man intuited the real Edwig Messinger.

Robert Friedman

Chapter 13

Okay, bottles of rum, scotch and cognac for Joe; rum, perfume, a tin of good coffee and a couple cartons of cigarettes for Toni; for Cheryl, violet water cologne. She already had packed away the two large dolls in Puerto Rican outfits and the metal snappers that looked like Puerto Rican *coquí* frogs along with the tee shirts, which she had bought for her granddaughter during the week. The liquor and cigarettes would be delivered, she was told, after she boarded the plane. She went to a bar next to the duty-free shop and had one, then two, then three glasses of scotch on the rocks.

What a day yesterday had been. She had missed the goddamn flight again! This time it was because of that maniac. They had reached the airport ten minutes after the plane left. Halfway there, they had to stop for gas and to get air in the tires. He had insisted the car would run out at any minute and that the tires were wobbly. She didn't believe him. When they arrived late at the airport, he slobbered over her with apologies and offered to pay for another night's stay for her at the guesthouse. She would pay her own way. She turned down an invitation to dinner, telling him she wasn't feeling well. Must have been that fried stuff they had for lunch at the roadside stands. "I'm gonna shower, then go to bed."

Then he told her that he would like her to work with him as a "consultant" on his project—whatever the hell that would have meant. He could not pay her much, but he was sure that the satisfaction she would get from the job, along with a livable salary, would be more than sufficient.

"I believe you would be a great addition to the project," he said. "Your people skills shine through."

Yeah, right.

She said she would go home first—she got another flight the next day at noon, which cost her fifty extra bucks—and discuss it with her family. Arrangements would have to be made. He nodded, slowly, like he was sympathizing with her —or that he was realizing her excuse was baloney. She didn't give a damn what he thought. She just wanted to get the hell home.

"I'll see you in the morning. I'll drive you to the airport."

"Yeah, sure," said Sally. "Just not too early."

"Nine," he said.

"Make it ten."

The next morning, Sally was out of the guesthouse with all her bags at eight. She took a taxi to the airport, four hours til flight time. She got coffee and a roll at a restaurant in the terminal, then checked her bags and went through security and to the duty-free shop.

Teamster Pete was pretty generous when he paid her for filling in for his secretary. He only came on to her once, the first day at the office, sliding his hand on her behind after he showed her around and brought her to his office. She told him she had "medical problems down below" and he let up for the rest of the time she worked there.

It was time to fly. Sally had an aisle seat, next to a middle-aged woman with short, straight, dyed blonde hair and heavy makeup. She wore a silky white blouse and designer jeans. The woman, Sally realized with a weird feeling, looked somewhat like her.

So nutso wanted her to work for him. That, of course, was ridiculous, out of the question. Well, he was a jerk, but his idea to help poor people was decent enough. Just because someone has so many human failings, doesn't mean he, or she, can't do kind and generous things.

It started deep in the pit of her stomach, then welled up into her heart. She saw Joe in her head, and then she knew she loved that guy! She still did. She had to get over her belief that they no longer wanted each other. She would stop thinking of herself. She couldn't wait to see him again, to hold him, to take care of him.

As the plane started rumbling down the runway, the woman sitting next to Sally reached into a pocket of her jeans and took out a string of silver rosary beads. On takeoff, she crossed herself, shut her eyes, fingered the beads, mumbled something. She opened her eyes as the jet continued to climb through a series of cloud banks. The plane dipped slightly, then slid upwards. The woman looked over at Sally, half-frightened, half-apologetic; then she gave a shaky smile. The jet cleared the clouds and climbed over a blue ocean.

The woman said: "I can't...I always...I never..."

"*No problema*," said Sally, patting the woman's hand that clutched the armrest between them. "We all got our hang-ups."

Chapter 14

The morning after the incident at the home of Ana and Luis Concepción, Bernardo's "nephew" Jorge had come to the guesthouse. He had apologized profusely for being the cause of the fight between Bernardo and Mauricio Pérez.

"You have nothing to apologize for," Bernardo told him.

"Yeah, well, I shouldn't have been over there. It was my presence that stirred up the whole thing," Jorge said.

"Nonsense," said Bernardo. "*I* was the one who lost my temper. I should know by now about...fellows like Mauricio."

"But he insulted you, Tío."

"Okay, so now it's over. Please tell your parents that I will pay for a new coffee table."

"Pérez already has had two new tables delivered this morning," Jorge said.

Bernardo nodded. It figured.

"Hey, Tío, let's forget it happened," Jorge said. "By the

way, will you be coming to the University next week when I give my talk on our recent trip to Cuba?"

"We'll see."

"I sure hope you do."

"Why?"

"Because I know I'll get the truth from you."

"The truth about what?"

"You know, what should be done by the people here about Cuba."

"I have no idea," said Bernardo.

"I do," said Jorge. "I'd like you to hear my proposal. It's going to be different from what you think. Maybe you'll even want to get involved again."

That's all I need, thought Bernardo.

"We'll see," he said.

Chapter 15

The Colibri Gallery on Cristo Street in Old San Juan was packed. Luigi Marrozzini, the Italian-born art dealer/gallery owner—short, svelte, a balding pate, a thick black mustache, immaculately dressed in a white linen suit, blue shirt and red-and-blue striped tie—greeted invited guests with an *abrazo,* holding his arms around the women longer. He pointed to a second room in the back of the gallery where drinks—wine, scotch, rum, vodka—were offered on a long table set up as a bar. The gallery-goers drank, laughed, spoke loudly, and occasionally looked at the more than twenty paintings on exhibit, fifteen of them new works by the artist Pablo Cruz Phillips.

A craggy faced Pablo stood somewhat defiantly against a wall in a corner near the bar, a scotch on the rocks jiggling slightly in his hand. He got nods from the people, and complements on his works. Those who tried to engage him in conversation got short, though not unpleasant, answers to their questions.

Approaching was Don Cisco, whom Pablo remembered meeting one tipsy evening at the bar of the Solimar Guesthouse —Perry, the bartender, had introduced them as the old man downed a Bromo-Seltzer. He had told Pablo then hat he admired his work. "Your paintings swirl from the head and onto the canvas and into the heart." Pablo remembered that.

He sort of warmed up to the old man who now said that he had read about the exhibition in the local newspaper, adding: "This is something I would never miss because I consider your work filling the gaps in our souls."

Pablo gave a warm smile and exchanged abrazos with the old guy.

Things got much touchier with Orestes Enrique Ortiz Del Valle, the very short, very opinionated art critic for the *Arte, Cultura, Et Al* weekly newspaper, read by residents with an interest in the arts and culture. The barely five-foot-tall Ortiz Del Valle was wearing a neck brace, which he had been doing for the past several months, after being thrown down a flight of stairs of an art gallery in Río Piedras by a local artist. The artist was reacting to a devastating Del Valle review of his one-man show. The works, Del Valle had written, were "shoddily wrought compositions with repetitive structural themes in which the artist's pretensions to achieve the purity of form and color of Malevich, Mondrian or

Reinhardt pathetically turn out to be utter failures."

The critic now looked up through his large, round, black-rimmed glasses at Pablo and announced: "Congratulations. You have apparently resolved your medieval fear of the abyss that prevented you from continuing to paint. But your new work, I must say, still shows that the maniacal morbidity of your vision, in composition and color, since you no longer appear to give value to the figure."

Pablo grunted.

"I do, however, like several of your abstracts," the critic continued, straining to keep his head at an angle so he could look at Pablo's face. "They have a special illusion created by those solid areas of color and the clearly defined texture— you've managed to transform them into areas of visual transparency. Those overlapping shapes create veils over the entire surface. I would say that..."

"Fuck off," Pablo said softly.

Ortiz Del Valle took off his glasses, wiped them on the hem of his long-sleeved, light-blue guayabera, put his glasses back on and shrugged, as though it was more important that he continue his critique than any reaction to what he was saying. "Malevich, Kandinsky, they were the ones we must compare your work to," he continued. "Your geometric vocabulary at times rivals their works, but you never forego the expressive content. That shows your command of the vocabulary of abstraction. It's just that you should soften your palette and..."

Pablo interrupted: "Look, I stopped doing figurative to focus on the act of painting itself. My recognizable forms were being submerged in abstractions of vivid colors. So I went abstract. That's it. Got it?"

Pablo tapped Ortiz Del Valle lightly on the top of his head, went to the bar for a refill. He drank the rum in a few gulps, put the glass down on the table, shook hands with the bartender and a disappointed Luigi, who said he hoped the artist would stick around for another hour or two. Pablo headed back to his apartment-studio.

He wasn't feeling bad about cutting out early. He really didn't give a damn if he sold any more paintings. Annie and Carlos had wanted him to show his new work at their exile gallery in New York. He was glad he had refused. Yeah, he was as exile as any exile could be. So? He didn't start painting again to let everyone know, including himself, how solidly solitary he was.

Well, he did. He *was* an exile from almost everything and everyone around him. But what *really* drove him was that other thing: that as long as he was alive, he had to paint.

Had to.

In Madrid, Sarah received rave reviews for her

Bernarda. *"¡Magnífico!"* declared El País; *"¡Tremendo!"* enthused ABC; *"¡Maravilloso!"* marveled El Mundo. The production was taken to Barcelona, where *Vanguardia's* critic Pau Roig called Sara's performance *"¡Majestuosa!"*

Sarah was overjoyed by her success. Lucas Carasquillo, the Spanish producer who arranged to bring her over for the Lorca Festival, fell hard for Sarah. He put her up in a Madrid apartment he owned (he lived just outside the city in Las Rozas with wife and three children). She insisted on paying rent, and Carasquillo charged her a nominal fee. For the first few months, she resisted his advances, but finally agreed to lovemaking, once in a great while.

She was at first eagerly caught up in the theater life of Madrid, yet soon realized that the crowd she hung with was little different than the actors, directors and writers in Puerto Rico.

Carasquillo helped cast Sarah mostly in revivals: as Blanche DuBois in *Un Tranvía llamado deseo,* as Martha in *¿Quién le teme a Virginia Woolf?*.

Been there, been there.

The truth was she missed her island, she missed her friends there, even missed Pablo...sort of. She stayed in Spain a year. When she returned to the island, she resumed seeing Pablo, once a week. She was overjoyed that he was painting again, but knew that each had to live a life on his and her own. She told Pablo so.

"Right," he said. "We'll stay apart...except when we're together."

Chapter 16

The day and many of the nights after that night of nights at the apartment, Margie visited Perry once more at his place of work. After the bar closed, Perry occasionally accompanied Margie to her apartment. But most nights, and now more and more often, he let her know he would be going to his own place.

"What's the matter, lover?" Margie asked after Perry's latest hemming and hawing and, finally, copping out. This time he couldn't make it because he had to get up early the next morning to look into taking the courses that would give him the credits to apply for the teaching job he *really* wanted.

Margie said: "Is our great romance over? Do I have to return to getting my kicks with *perico?"*

"Hey, no, I'm sorry. I'm really, truly sorry. It's nothing to do with you. It's me. I still got issues. I…"

"Hey, man, *fuck* the issues. I can cook you a great late dinner and we can just sit around and read and talk."

"Yeah, sure. Well..."

"Well?"

"Yeah, well, I appreciate..."

"I don't want appreciation. You helped me as much, if not more, than I helped you. I'm off the drugs and I work steady as a waitress, and nothing more. I even dig cooking those midnight dinners."

"I see what you're saying. But I don't think I'll be coming over to your place anymore. It's not what I can do anymore."

"Screw you," said Margie.

"Yeah, fuck me. I'm really an asshole."

"You're acting like one now, even though basically you're a decent guy. What you need is...what you just need..."

"Yeah?"

"Oh, who the hell knows? Gimme another rum on the rocks."

Margie drank. The ice cubes clinked. "You found another woman? Or maybe a young boy?"

"No. No one else."

"Then?"

"Well, whenever I'm with you, I feel...I don't know... sort of nervous. No, it's more—like I don't like myself."

"So? Join the club."

"Yeah, but..."

"But, but. Okay, we're being honest here, right? Nobody is bullshitting nobody. In your own dumb way, you helped me see something deeper about myself."

"Good or bad?"

"More important, something deeper, truer. Maybe not yet who I really am, but who I'm not. Didn't you learn anything about yourself?"

Perry shrugged. "I ain't that introspective. I just know I got problems."

"You want to know the truth? We're both pretty surface people. But we both want to treat people, and be treated by them, decently. Maybe from that comes the good things in life. Maybe there ain't much more in life—except for a good book."

Margie leaned forward on her stool. "C'mere."

Perry leaned over the bar. Margie gently put her hands on his cheeks, kissed him deeply. Perry softly bit her tongue and her lips, then pulled his head back.

"Thanks, lover," Margie said.

"I hope you realize that you are a wonderful person, " Perry said.

He gave Margie that fruity wave as she left.

Robert Friedman

Chapter 17

He finally reached Willy, who after bitching and moaning about the just-opened goddamn Costco in the mall near his store, said he would send Burt a check for $500. Burt got a dishwasher's job at the Caribe Hilton Hotel and joined the Hotel Workers Union, Local 610, a requirement to get the job. He was pissed that he had no choice, but then saw himself leading a strike one day against the goddamn millionaires who owned the tourist hotels.

He rented a room in a dingy hotel in the Old City that was filled with Haitians and Dominicans. The room was half the size of the one he had at the Solimar Guesthouse, barely enough space for a bed, a dresser and his papers. But, what the hell, he was just a couple of blocks from the courthouse, a short bus ride to the hotel and within walking distance for his weekly visit with Luz.

Guess what? He actually *liked* his Haitian neighbors. Once, when he got dengue fever and was laid up for a week,

Jean-Claude, the guy who lived in the next room, cooked up meals for him in the community kitchen and brought the food to his room, always with a big smile, which was irritating, but the old guy's heart was in the right place.

Everyone in the hotel kitchen knew that Burt was the best pots and pans man they had ever worked with. Besides the usual soaps and scrubs for the manual cleaning, he did tricks with salt, vinegar and cream of tartar that made the pots and pans gleam like new.

One Friday night, as he was licking one of Luz's nipples and she looked down on him with what seemed like a genuine, motherly, forehead-creased smile, he suddenly stopped, took her in his arms and said: "You wanna live with me? I got a regular salary now. We'll rent a house."

The creases in Luz's forehead deepened. "You kiddin' me, *papi*?"

"No, well, yeah…well…"

He did and he didn't mean it.

Her smile turned to something else. Her eyes softened. "I say *gracias* but no. I couldn't. I'm goin' home soon, where is my daughter. I send money to her school in Venezeula. But, *gracias, mi amor.*"

"That's okay," Bert said. "While you're here, we'll still see each other once a week."

"*Claro,*" said Luz.

Where did *that* come from? He couldn't, wouldn't, live with anyone else.

But maybe he could give it a try.

He was *really* starting to get creepy, Burt thought, then put his mouth to Luz's nipple again.

Robert Friedman

Chapter 18

After another few weeks of reading *The Times* and experiencing scary, crazy day-and-nightmares, Fred Anderson returned to New York. Right after he arrived at Kennedy, he called Kathy. He invited her for dinner at Widows of the World.

"I have to get a babysitter," she said.

"Please do," he said.

They decided at dinner that he would come home again. He would give Wall Street another go.

Kathy said: "I missed you. I'm glad you're back."

So you can bitch again about everything I do, he thought.

Shut up! He told himself. Think good thoughts.

Robert Friedman

Chapter 19

Protestors gathered outside the University building where a discussion about *El Bloqueo,* The U. S. blockade of Cuba, would be held. The protestors tried to shout each other down. *"¡Cuba, sí, yanqui, no!"* clashed with *"¡Castro, comunista sucio!"*

Bernardo made his way down the aisle of the theater where he had seen the University film club's showings of *Memories of Underdevelopment, The Battle of Algiers, Z* and films by Bunuel, Fellini, Kurosawa, Bergman. The theater was packed and noisy. Bernardo found an aisle seat in the third row, far off to the side. He decided to attend the event out of solidarity—with Jorge. At a long table on the stage sat three young men, including Jorge, and three gray-haired professors.

Two students and one professor argued that the blockade was the way to go (loud boos, catcalls). The other members of the panel, including Jorge, countered that the U.

263

S. policy hurt both the people trying to survive in Cuba and the image abroad of the U. S., already seen as an oppressor and a big bully (cheers and stamping of feet).

Then Jorge said: "I have recently returned from a trip to Cuba, where I helped with the sugar harvest (whistles, cheers). I was born in Cuba, and was sent out of the country in *Operación Peter Pan.* I was eventually adopted and brought to this wonderful island from Florida by my new parents. My mother is Puerto Rican, all the way (cheers), and my father is a Cuban who actually fought for the revolution before he became disillusioned and left the island. Most of my life, despite my father's beliefs and wishes, I have supported the revolution (cheers, whistles and catcalls).

"So I have experienced, to a small degree perhaps, but more than others, both sides of the debate, the arguments the irrational and rational policies and hatreds, how it could pit family members against family members and friends against friends, etcetera, etcetera.

"Now, for what it's worth, here's what I believe: Cuba should be free of U. S. control, political or economic. U. S. business interests should stay out of the country, unless they're invited in. Education and health care should continue to be free and the people should be able to start businesses and run their own farms. The revolution is a historical fact. And people should have the right to vote. Only the Cuban people, and not Washington, have the right to decide who leads their country. If the people vote against Fidel, he should give up his power. If they want Fidel to continue to lead the country, the U. S. should butt out."

Shouts of *"¡Mentiras!* Lies!"* broke out from a group of five or six guys standing in the back of the auditorium. One of them opened the rear door and a dozen others came in wielding clubs. They moved down the aisles, smashing the backs of seats. There was shouting, screaming, fistfights.

Then, a gunshot.

A half-second of stunned silence, as though all air and sound had been sucked out of the auditorium, followed by shrieks, cries, ducking under seats, scrambling for the exits.

Jorge slumped forward, his head hitting the table.

Bernardo jumped out of his seat, ran down the side aisle, up steps and onto the stage. He lifted Jorge from his chair and held him in his arms. Blood was coming from the side of Jorge's head. Bernardo looked around, realized only he and Jorge were on stage. He was going to take off his shirt to staunch the blood when a young woman came running up the side steps carrying a first-aid kit. Bernardo dug into the kit, bundled together gauze pads and held them against Jorge's wound. When the blood flow slowed, he taped gauze over the pads, shouting for someone to get an ambulance. People were frozen, then running, shouting, pushing, hugging, crying.

Minutes went by and no help appeared. Bernardo, holding Jorge in his arms, pulled him up out of his chair and with the help of a young man who appeared on the steps to the stage, brought Jorge down to a side door. He carried Jorge the one hundred yards to the parking lot and put him in the back seat of his car. Jorge was still alive, moaning. Blood seeping through the soaked gauze on the side of his head. Bernardo opened the trunk and took out a clean towel from the gym bag for his racquetball sessions at Casa Cuba. He wrapped the towel around Jorge's head. Jorge blinked. He laid Jorge across the back seat, propping up his head with a sweatshirt and a rain jacket he also had stored in the trunk. He got behind the wheel and tore across the campus. A guard at the gate on a walkie-talkie pushed out an arm toward the car and shouted at Bernardo to stop. Bernardo swerved the car around the guard and barreled through the half-open gate and sped across Río Piedras toward the government medical center, going through a light as a bus driver shouted obscenities at him.

Bernardo walked up and down a hallway in Centro Médico, breathing heavily. He went to a waiting room, sat on the edge of a green plastic sofa, looked down, rubbed his forehead. His adopted nephew was being operated on. Bernardo stood again, went to a hallway phone, called the home of Ana and Luis. There was no answer. He returned to the waiting room, paced, sat, paced.

After forever, he was told that despite a severe injury to Jorge's brain, he would survive.

Chapter 20

It was only mild indigestion when he awoke. He moved his bowels, only slightly, then shaved, showered, put on his black linen suit, white shirt and gray tie. A quick shot of warmed-over Cuban coffee. He would eat at the cafeteria during the first recess. The pain in the middle of Luis Concepción's stomach remained. He felt a momentary light-headedness as he pulled his Lincoln Continental from the garage. The car was fully air-conditioned, but he began to sweat more than usual as he drove to the Hato Rey courthouse.

The courtroom was close to freezing, yet his sweating continued. Pain shot through the top of his chest and into his jaw. Still, he decided he would begin arguing the case. He owed it to the ten homeowners in the newly gated community in Guaynabo who filed the class-action against Advanced Construction. Leaking roofs, flooding basements, cracked foundations, faulty wiring, constant electric outages. How the hell could anyone live like that? He sure as hell would get these people some relief.

As he began his opening statement, the stomach pains returned in full force, then shot deeply into his chest and he crumbled to the floor and was rushed by ambulance to the government medical center. He was brought to the emergency room, then, after a time—how many hours?—was wheeled into a room in the coronary care unit on the second floor. Luis was one floor below the neurosciences intensive care unit where he had previously visited Jorge.

Bernardo took Ana, who didn't drive, to and from the hospital. He brought her in the mornings, stayed a few hours to visit both Jorge and Luis, then returned to the guesthouse. On the nights Ana didn't sleep over in the lounge chair in her husband's room, Bernardo went back to the hospital to pick her up and drive her home. He had a cocktail with her, then made dinner for his children. Bernardo also gave rides to and from the hospital to Yvonne, Jorge's wife, often driving her to the daycare center to pick up Luisito. Bernardo then drove them to Ana's house, where Yvonne and her son were staying.

A few days after the incident at the University, authorities announced the arrest of a highly troubled nineteen-year-old part-time student, who was said to have confessed that he shot Jorge "for Cuba and for freedom." The media reported that the suspect had no known connections to any pro-Castro or anti-Castro group. Both sides blamed the other for putting the gun into the shooter's hand.

After being released from the hospital, Luis, in his office reviewing papers in the homeowners' case against the construction company, suffered another heart attack, this one fatal.

Bernardo helped Ana arrange the funeral. Many members of the Cuban community, as well as fellow lawyers and two judges, attended.

Two weeks later, the funeral and burial for Don Cisco was held at the Old San Juan cemetery, alongside the seaside slum of La Perla. Several of Don Cisco's former students and fellow teachers were in attendance, as well as one of his ex-wives and three of his five children, their spouses and children. The families stayed at the Solimar Guesthouse, where Don Cisco had passed away in his sleep.

His body had been discovered by Marta Silva. While he no longer sat for his portrait—even though Marta had not yet finished it—she continued to work on it. They had resumed their Sunday morning walks. When he had not appeared in the patio where they met for their walks, and Marta had gone to his room and had knocked on the door, which Don Cisco seldom locked. She called out as she entered the room. Don Cisco lay on his back on the room's pullout couch-bed, his arms stretched out at his sides as though he had just plopped down, exhausted. His mouth was open. There was a quizzical look on his face.

Bernardo transported Marta to the cemetery in his car. They drove up Calle Norzagaray, past Fort San Cristobal, along Boulevard Del Valle, the pastel-colored colonial houses on one side and the 16th Century Spanish walls on the other. Bernardo turned the car down a narrow road by the wall, went through a short tunnel and arrived at the grave-packed cemetery. Don Cisco's open grave lay among the many stone-carved angels peering at the ocean and up to the sky.

While ample tears were shed by the mourners, Marta Silva could not cry. She did not know why. She had become closer to Don Cisco than she had ever been to any man. One weekend, they had even had sex, of a kind. She admired his mind, loved his consideration of her and his companionship. She would miss him greatly, but she could not cry.

Back at the guesthouse, Perry served snacks and drinks to the mourners. Bernardo sat at a table on the patio with Marta and with Don Cisco's former wife, the one who, Don Cisco had told Marta, left him after telling him he had too many other interests to ever return her deep love for him. She had come to the funeral from Jamaica, where she said she was born, had left at an early age to live in London and New York, then returned to a few years ago. She was a small, very thin woman. Marta felt buxom by comparison. The ex-wife, who introduced herself as Lady Miranda, had beige-colored skin that was incredibly smooth for what had to be her seventy or so years. Her gray hair was braided and piled on top of her angular head. Her long flowing dress was white. Her eyes, behind wire-rimmed glasses, were a light brown.

Lady Miranda said her profession was that of clairvoyant. Speaking in a slightly British accent, she said: "I use no ouija boards, no crystal balls. As the word 'clairvoyant' indicates, my principal 'power,' if you will, comes from the ability to see clearly. I perceive the future through my understanding of the past. It is the process of reasoning rather than mysticism that allows me to see what is to come. I have been gifted to have the power to reason in this often unreasonable world."

Bernardo kept nodding. Marta wondered why Lady Miranda was offering this advertisement of her "powers."

Lady Miranda turned to Marta. "You are in the arts," she said.

"Well, I'm...I'm a saleswoman. I sell perfume at a department store. But...well..."

"Yes, I know," said Lady Miranda. "You would much rather be painting."

Quick blinks from Marta. "How do you...?"

"Your facial expressions, your demeanor. You are an artist."

Marta bit her thumbnail.

Seeming to change the subject, Lady Miranda said: "You know, my former husband, he believed in reincarnation."

"Well," Marta said. "He told me he did not rule it out."

"He whole-heartedly believed. And he will be back," said Lady Miranda. "Rest assured."

Marta blinked. She looked over to Bernardo. He smiled, shrugged, drank his cognac.

"Your Don Cisco, who once was my love, will be back —through you. You will bring him back to life."

Marta frowned. What was this woman talking about?

"Yes, you will finish the portrait. And you will have captured the true Don Cisco. So true, he will be among us once more."

Marta bit down hard on her lip. "How do you...?"

Lady Miranda actually winked at Marta, then patted Marta's hands, which were folded in her lap.

"Reason foretells the future," said Lady Miranda with a dreamy smile, then finished off her Jamaican rum on the rocks. "I have to go back to my room and pack. My plane for Kingston leaves soon." She shook Bernardo's hand and tightly held Marta's hand. "I believe you are on the way to becoming a true artist." She winked again, let go of Marta's hand and left.

Marta gave Bernardo a puzzled, yet satisfied, look. She

realized that Lady Miranda had clearly seen into her soul—as well as discussed her with Don Cisco in telephone calls.

Edwig Messinger sat alone at a table drinking an on-the-house cognac. Bernardo passed the table and the two men nodded at one another. "Please join me," said Edwig. "I just knew Don Cisco for a short time, but I found him a wonderful gentleman. Very intelligent, well-read."

Then he told Bernardo that he would be moving in the coming weeks. "I believe I told you about my plans to dedicate the land I hope to once again regain for the poor living out there. Well, I have decided that I will move out there with them. Don Cisco certainly understood. He said my idea was 'noble' and my heart"—Edwig tapped his chest—"is 'in the right place'. I will always remember those words. We only met very briefly once or twice. But I will remember Don Cisco's words."

Bernardo nodded. There were tears in Edwig Messinger's eyes. He wiped his eyes with a green silk bandana he took from his back pocket, and finished his cognac.

Bernardo excused himself, went to the bar and told Perry to keep filling Messinger's cognac glass.

Pablo and Ana had also attended the funeral. Pablo remembered that the old man had come to his exhibit some weeks ago, which was for him a sort-of rebirth, so the least he could do was pay his respects to the old guy. When Pablo had told Ana about the old guy's comments at his show, about the paintings swirling from his head onto the canvas and into the heart, she had replied: "That man had understood your art. He understood your being."

Pablo nodded. Close enough.

Chapter 21

Five months later, Jorge was released from a therapy center. While in the hospital, he twice underwent surgery on his skull and brain. He was able to move his arms and legs and to speak, very slowly. Bernardo spent hours each day helping Jorge with his physical therapy.

Finally, the day arrived when Jorge could walk slowly down the beach into the ocean, up to his knees. He smiled broadly at Bernardo. "The w-water," Jorge said. "It feels g-great, Tío."

They were soon joined by Bernardo's children, Anita and Pablito, and by Jorge's little son, Luisito, who held Anita's hand. They all rode the swells, and then, when Luisito dived into a breaking wave, Jorge followed. There were cheers all around, including from Ana and Jorge's wife, Yvonne, both of whom were standing at the water's edge, tears in their eyes.

Not too long after, Jorge was well-enough to join a group seeking dialogue with Cuba and wrote position papers and press releases for them. Bernardo attended a few of the group's meetings. But he soon realized, more strongly than ever, that exile from politics was, for him, a permanent condition. Considering what his family and friends had been through, this saddened him deeply.

After dinner and a movie, Bernardo and Ana return to the guesthouse and sit at a patio table. Perry brings them Rémy Martins. Bernardo reaches down and softly runs his fingers across the back of Ana's hand. They smile, drink their cognac, then Ana excuses herself. She goes to the countertop jukebox at the end of the bar. She puts in a coin and Nat "King" Cole begins to sing in Spanish about green eyes. Ana comes back and holds out her hand. "Time to dance," she says.

Bernardo stands, somewhat reluctantly, then turns a short grimace into another smile. He puts his arm around Ana. They dance.

As Nat Cole sings, Ana joins in, first in Spanish, then in in English.

"Your green eyes with their soft lights;

"Your eyes that promise sweet nights

"Bring to my soul a longing, a thirst for love divine.

"In dreams I seem to hold you, to find you and enfold you;

"Our lips meet, and our hearts, too, with a thrill so sublime…"

"Sorry, but my eyes are brown," says Bernardo.

"So are mine," says Ana. *"No importa.* It does not matter."

They dance and Nat "King" Cole's softly hypnotic voice slides into his soul and Ana's sweet cinnamon scent glides through his nostrils and taps at his heart and Bernardo realizes where his true ties to life lie.

Robert Friedman

About the Author

Robert Friedman was a reporter, columnist and city editor for the *San Juan Star* in Puerto Rico for more than 20 years, and was the newspaper's Washington correspondent until it folded in 2009. While in Puerto Rico, he was also a special correspondent for the New York *Daily News*. Friedman is the author of four published novels about Puerto Rico—*The Surrounding Sea*, *Under a Dark Sun*, *Shadow of the Fathers* and *Caribbean Dreams*. In his fiction, he has explored the colorful and often struggling lives of island residents who try to cope, both personally and politically, with the highly ambivalent relationship between the U.S. and Puerto Rico. Born and bred in the Bronx, New York, he now lives in Silver Spring, Md.

For more on the author, go to Amazon.com: RobertFriedman and/or contact him at friedmanro@gmail.com.

Robert Friedman

If you enjoyed *Island Wildlife,* consider these other fine books from Aignos Publishing:

The Dark Side of Sunshine by Paul Guzzo
Happy that it's Not True by Carlos Aleman
Cazadores de Libros Perdidos by German William Cabasssa Barber [Spanish]
The Desert and the City by Derek Bickerton
The Overnight Family Man by Paul Guzzo
There is No Cholera in Zimbabwe by Zachary M. Oliver
John Doe by Buz Sawyers
The Piano Tuner's Wife by Jean Yamasaki Toyama
Nuno by Carlos Aleman
An Aura of Greatness: Reflections on Governor John A. Burns by Brendan P. Burns
Polonio Pass by Doc Krinberg
Iwana by Alvaro Leiva
University and King by Jeffrey Ryan Long
The Surreal Adventures of Dr. Mingus by Jesus Richard Felix Rodriguez
Letters by Buz Sawyers
In the Heart of the Country by Derek Bickerton
El Camino De Regreso by Maricruz Acuna [Spanish]
Diego in Two Places by Carlos Aleman
Prepositions by Jean Yamasaki Toyama
Deep Slumber of Dogs by Doc Krinberg
Saddam's Parrot by Jim Currie
Beneath Them by Natalie Roers
Chang the Magic Cat by A. G. Hayes
Illegal by E. M. Duesel

Coming Soon:
The Winter Spider by Doc Krinberg
The Princess in My Head by J. G. Matheny

Aignos Publishing | an imprint of Savant Books and Publications
www.aignospublishing.com

Island Wildlife: Exiles, Expats, and Exotic Others

as well as these other fine books from Savant Books and Publications:

Essay, Essay, Essay by Yasuo Kobachi
Aloha from Coffee Island by Walter Miyanari
Footprints, Smiles and Little White Lies by Daniel S. Janik
The Illustrated Middle Earth by Daniel S. Janik
Last and Final Harvest by Daniel S. Janik
A Whale's Tale by Daniel S. Janik
Tropic of California by R. Page Kaufman
Tropic of California (the companion music CD) by R. Page Kaufman
The Village Curtain by Tony Tame
Dare to Love in Oz by William Maltese
The Interzone by Tatsuyuki Kobayashi
Today I Am a Man by Larry Rodness
The Bahrain Conspiracy by Bentley Gates
Called Home by Gloria Schumann
Kanaka Blues by Mike Farris
First Breath edited by Z. M. Oliver
Poor Rich by Jean Blasiar
The Jumper Chronicles by W. C. Peever
William Maltese's Flicker by William Maltese
My Unborn Child by Orest Stocco
Last Song of the Whales by Four Arrows
Perilous Panacea by Ronald Klueh
Falling but Fulfilled by Zachary M. Oliver
Mythical Voyage by Robin Ymer
Hello, Norma Jean by Sue Dolleris
Richer by Jean Blasiar
Manifest Intent by Mike Farris
Charlie No Face by David B. Seaburn
Number One Bestseller by Brian Morley
My Two Wives and Three Husbands by S. Stanley Gordon
In Dire Straits by Jim Currie
Wretched Land by Mila Komarnisky
Chan Kim by Ilan Herman
Who's Killing All the Lawyers? by A. G. Hayes
Ammon's Horn by G. Amati
Wavelengths edited by Zachary M. Oliver
Almost Paradise by Laurie Hanan
Communion by Jean Blasiar and Jonathan Marcantoni
The Oil Man by Leon Puissegur
Random Views of Asia from the Mid-Pacific by William E. Sharp
The Isla Vista Crucible by Reilly Ridgell
Blood Money by Scott Mastro

Robert Friedman

Island Wildlife: Exiles, Expats, and Exotic Others